MW01146817

Dawn's Gentle Light

Renee Riva

Renee Riva

Copyright © 2017 Renee Riva

Pink Heart Press

All rights reserved.

ISBN-13: 9781975813772

For my first and favorite writing teacher, Colleen Reece, who taught me the ropes, set an example of writing with dignity, and encouraged me to get back on the horse and ride again.
And for Yulia, my Russian twin.

Bickleton, Washington
1979

The farming town of Bickleton lay beneath a blanket of snow. Pine boughs and holly framed the front window of Buck's Hardware on Main. Across the street, a single strand of Christmas lights blinked on and off at Ruby's Come Back Café; the only café in town. Twelve-year-old Clara stared out the frosted window from a corner booth. She sipped hot chocolate while her parents landed the final blow to her formerly happy life. With the simple stroke of a pen, Ella and Nicholas Bradley signed their names, and sealed her doom.

"Thank you, both," the real estate lady concluded. "Here are the keys to your new home. I hope you will all be very happy here." The woman glanced at Clara with the same smile she had given Clara's parents, receiving a blank stare in return. "I'm sure you will love it here."

Clara returned her comment with an icy glare.

Clara's mother shot her a disapproving look.

"Yes, Ma'am," Clara mumbled. It had taken all year to make friends at junior high school in Oregon. She'd finally made Cheer Club after months of practice. Now she had no one to cheer with and nothing to cheer about.

Clara climbed into the backseat of the family station wagon beside her brother, Max. At age three, he was oblivious to the cruel fate handed down to them by their parents, and continued his annoying chatter. Clara stared out the car window in silence as they passed acres of endless, white nothingness. A tear rolled down her cheek, unnoticed by her parents.

"Here we are," her father announced, far too jovial. "Our new home, sweet home."

Clara's eyes darted from a small white farmhouse to a weathered red barn, then across the street to a ... "Oh, my gosh... is that what I think it is?"

"What's that, dear?" Her mother asked in a cheerful voice.

"Don't tell me we live across the street from a creepy old cemetery?"

"Oh," her dad perked up, "that happens to be a very interesting, historical landmark. It's one of the oldest cemeteries in Washington State, dating as far back as...."

"Hold on," Clara cut in. "You seriously moved us across the street from a haunted graveyard with century-old dead bodies and you're proud of it?" Clara bolted from the car. "My family has lost it!" She marched toward the front door, gearing up for whatever other horrors were in store for her.

The movers had already come and gone, leaving boxes piled in every room as designated. Nicholas Bradley's employer had provided the movers as part of his job incentive package. The Eastern Washington Land Waste Management crew was eager to get Nicholas on board as soon as possible. He was equally eager to get started. Recent cutbacks in the Oregon plant had put him at risk of being laid off. He jumped at the chance for the transfer. For once he would have a short commute to work. He could actually see the land waste plant on the horizon from his home—another fact his daughter found disconcerting.

Clara hid in her room, refusing to come out for dinner. "I just want to go to sleep!" she yelled through her closed door.

Her mother patiently endured the drama that came with moving her pre-adolescent daughter from Oregon to Washington. She prayed it would eventually turn out okay. As any mother would, she had her doubts.

Morning came with the sun shining through Clara's sheer white curtains. She lazily opened her eyes, and then quickly shut them again, remembering where she was. The despair returned. Thank goodness it was Saturday. She'd at least been spared the trauma of starting a new school that morning.

Clara got out of bed, pulled back her curtains, and peered out at the white rolling hills. From her second story window, she had a bird's eye view of the cemetery. Out of the stillness, she saw someone. A woman. A short woman in a heavy wool coat and bright scarf. She made the sign of the cross standing before a grave marker. It not only caught Clara's attention, it made her curious.

The woman placed her gloved hand on the name engraved on the wood cross, then turned to go. Clara's gaze followed her out the rusted gate and along the road, until she turned toward the cottage on her left. She followed her along the white picket fence, through the rose arbor, and up the walk until the door closed behind her. "I guess I'm not the only one who lives next to a creepy cemetery," Clara muttered. Something in that statement gave her a strange sense of comfort.

Clara slipped into her snow boots, grabbed her coat, and crept quietly down the narrow staircase, hoping to escape without waking up her family. She walked down the driveway to the road, then crossed to the entrance of the Bickleton Cemetery. The rusty iron gate squeaked as she passed through. Clara glanced at the snow-covered crosses on the small hillside. The thought of frozen dead bodies below sent a shiver down her spine. A red rose caught her eye and drew her to where the old women had stood. Snow had been recently brushed from the name on the face of the large wood cross.

Pavel Petrovich Uvarov
1896—1975

As she neared the grave, an intense fragrance filled the air, but glancing down, there was only one red rose at the foot of the cross. How could a single rose emit such a strong fragrance? Clara stared at the name for the longest time. A gentle peace fell over her the way snow falls without a sound. She felt no fear or dread being in this cemetery alone. Only peace. That surprised her.

~

Clara spent the day arranging her new bedroom. Apart from her canopy bed, the main attraction was the framed bulletin board covered in photographs. She'd spent hours selecting pictures from a shoebox of pictures of the friends she'd made at Trenton Junior High, most of them from Cheer Club.

Every so often Clara found herself peering out her window at the cemetery. For some reason she could not get the old woman out of her mind. More so, she could not stop wondering about Pavel. He was born a century before her, and when she stood beside his grave she sensed something she could only describe as goodness.

Clara awoke Sunday morning hoping the whole move was one long nightmare. She sat up and glanced out her second story window to make sure. Yep. Still in Bickleton, and the cemetery was still there. So was the lady she'd seen the morning before.

Clara could hardly dress fast enough. She tucked her long, strawberry blonde hair into her knit hat, grabbed her coat, then rushed downstairs and out the back door. She hurried across the street, slowed a bit as she approached the old gate, then slipped through.

Now that Clara was there, she wasn't sure what to do. She felt as if she was intruding on a sacred moment and found herself unable to move. As the woman turned, she looked a bit startled, then her eyes softened. "Hello," the woman said, calmly.

"Hello." Clara wasn't sure what to say next.

"Do you live nearby?" the woman asked. She had a strong accent.

"There," Clara pointed across the street.

"Oh, your family bought the Johnson's old place?" She smiled.

"Yes. I'm Clara Bradley."

"Clara." The woman nodded. "I am Tetushka. That's a Russian name for Auntie, or, in my case, a nice way of including an old woman in the lives of children. I have no children or grandchildren of my own, but some of the children at my church have claimed me as their Tetushka. That's what everyone calls me now."

Clara smiled back. She couldn't help glancing at the cross a few feet from them. "I was wondering if you could tell me..." Clara felt nervous, but determined to know. "Who is Pavel?"

Tetushka sighed. "Pavel was many things to many people. But it is far too cold to tell you about him here." Tetushka pushed back her sleeve and glanced at her watch. "I must leave for church now, but come to my house tomorrow, and we will have tea. I live there," she pointed at the cottage at the edge of the cemetery. "Tell your Mama to come, too."

"Okay," Clara nodded. "We'll come tomorrow after school."

~

Uncertain what to wear to school, Clara decided on the outfit she bought with her birthday money; a pair of faded jeans and a pink thermal top. She pulled on her boots, grabbed her coat and headed for the kitchen.

"I'll need to go with you to the office this morning and make sure they have you enrolled," her mother cautioned.

Oh great. What better way to stand out than to have my mother walk me through the halls. "Then can we go early before the whole school arrives and sees me?"

"As soon as I get your brother dressed. He'll need to come too, since your father already left for work."

Perfect. Can it get any more embarrassing? Clara grabbed her pop tart from the toaster and waited impatiently for her Welcoming Committee to get ready.

"Okay, we're all set," her mother announced, as if they were heading out to do something enjoyable.

Just as Clara feared, the school busses pulled up the minute she stepped out of the car with her mother and little brother in tow. She intentionally stayed a few paces behind them to the office, but got the stare-down from students anyway. In such a small school, she felt like an elephant in a circus tent. Clara stood to one side, allowing her mother and the office lady to hash over the details of her ruined life. No doubt they were plotting to make sure she had no classes she was even remotely interested in. By the time they were done, the bell was ringing for her first class.

"Would you like me to show you to your class?" the lady with the cat-eye glasses offered.

"Um, no thank you; just point me in the right direction. I should be okay," Clara replied.

"I'll see you after school, honey," her mother said. I'll pick you up out front. We'll have to get the bus route figured out later this week."

Clara gave her mom a quick nod, and headed toward her first class.

First period: no one spoke to her—only stared.

Second period: P.E., but she didn't have the attire to suit up so she just watched from the sidelines as the class ran drills.

Third period: a boy picked up her pencil for her, then the girl next to him glared at Clara. Fortunately, they started watching a historical documentary in the dark. If people were staring, she couldn't see them.

By lunch, the thought of eating alone was unbearable so she went to the library and ate her sandwich behind a bookshelf.

By the time school was out, Clara was almost glad to see her mother and little brother. They were the only friendly faces she'd seen all day. Passing by the cemetery, she remembered the invitation she'd received the day before. "Oh, Mom, I told the lady across the street from us that I'd come over for tea today. She said to bring you too, to meet her."

Her mother looked puzzled. "What lady are you talking about? I didn't realize you'd met any of the neighbors."

Clara avoided the direct gaze. "I met her in the cemetery and she invited me for tea today. She's really old with an accent. Her name is Tetushka. That's Auntie in Russian."

Ella looked uneasy, knowing nothing about this woman her daughter had befriended. It wasn't like Clara to interact with strangers—especially the way she'd been behaving recently. On the other hand, she didn't want to discourage Clara from getting to know her new neighbors. "I suppose I could stop in for a moment, but I need to get Max home for a nap soon."

Clara pointed out the house beside the cemetery. They pulled into the drive beside the cottage. As Clara rang the bell, the woman opened the door. "Well, you have come, haven't you?" She looked pleased.

"Yes, and I brought my mom and little brother to meet you, too." Clara turned and introduced them. "This is my mom, Ella, and my brother, Max."

The two women greeted each other warmly, then Tetushka invited them in. "Come, sit down." She showed them into her small, tidy living room, offering them the two love-sized sofas, then started toward the kitchen. "I will bring some tea and sweets for us."

Clara glanced around at the wood shelves filled with painted lacquer boxes of beautiful fairytale images. In one corner of the room hung very old paintings of Jesus and Mary along with a number of faces she didn't recognize; perhaps some of the Apostles.

"These must be from Russia," her mother whispered.

Tetushka returned with a silver tray of delicate tea cups and a variety of cookies on a small glass plate. She placed the tea cups beneath the spigot on a large brass tea kettle of some sort. Hot tea poured from its spout into the cups.

Before taking a seat, Tetushka poured a cup for Ella and Clara, then presented Max with a white powdered cookie. "Now then," she said, as she settled into an overstuffed chair by the fire, "I'm so glad you've come. I was happy to hear a young family was moving in across from me, and here you are."

"Thank you for inviting us," Ella replied. "Clara tells me your name means Auntie."

"Yes. I am Tetushka to my church family." She smiled sweetly at Clara.

In spite of a few missing teeth, Clara thought it was a beautiful smile. Recalling that Tetushka had no family, Clara dismissed the idea that Pavel was her husband. She sensed her mother relaxing, approving of the older woman.

It wasn't long before Max got restless and ambled toward some stacking dolls, hands out. "I think I'd better get your brother down for a nap before too long or he'll never sleep tonight." Ella rose, intercepted Max before disaster struck, and thanked Tetushka for her kindness. Tetushka saw them out. She obviously had a calming effect on her mother. There were few strangers she was comfortable leaving her children with after knowing them for only ten minutes.

"Now, then, Clara, you wanted to know about Pavel."

Clara nodded, eager to hear what she had to say.

"The best way for me to tell you who Pavel was, is to let him tell you himself."

Clara was taken aback. "B-but, isn't he... dead?"

"Yes, but he lives on in his stories. You see, Pavel was a *skazochnik*, a storyteller. He told and wrote beautiful stories. They say the heart of a writer will come through his work. He wrote many stories, but his most beautiful story is one I am working on right now. It's about two young friends named Nina and Pasha. I believe someone your age might enjoy this story. It was written as samizdat; a form of secret publishing during Soviet times when this type of literature was forbidden."

"Oh, I love to read," Clara replied, "Could I read it?"

Tetushka smiled indulgently. "It's written in Russian, but I began translating it into English, hoping one day to share it with others. I haven't gotten very far but maybe you could help me. If you would like to read while I write, it will motivate me to keep going, knowing you are waiting for the next chapter."

"You mean read it here, like a chapter at a time?"

"Yes, if you don't mind. You can also let me know if I misinterpret anything."

"I would love to—it's much quieter here without my little brother." Clara loved the feel of being away from home in this cozy room by the fire, with warm tea and cookies.

"Wonderful. That will encourage me to finish translating Pavel's book. And by the end, I think you will understand the heart of Pavel Petrovich Uvarov."

Clara nodded. She loved unusual stories, and was fascinated with the thought of being the first one to read this Russian story in English.

Tetushka opened the cover of her three-ring binder. Inside were pages of beautifully handwritten script. "To give you an idea of what it's about, the story takes place in a small fishing town in Russia, in the year 1908. It begins with nine-year-old Nina, who was the only survivor in her family after typhoid fever passed through her town. Her family had once owned a nice home in St. Petersburg, but Nina is now left with her poor, elderly grandmother. The story is called *ZORKA*; meaning; Early Dawn. It will cover a span of about eight years as Nina is growing up—not year by year—but her most significant years."

Tetushka took out the first chapter handwritten in English, and carefully handed it to Clara, who received it with eager, but gentle hands. She settled back near the fire and began to read....

Renee Riva

Zorka

Renee Riva

Part 1

Rybatskaya, Russia
1908

The small fishing town of Rybatskaya was looking forward to an unexpected event at their fall festival. Dasha Bukovsky, a St. Petersburg ballerina, had come to spend her summer by the sea, visiting relatives at their summer dacha. She was so fond of the quaint theatrical clubhouse, that Miss Bukovsky had offered to direct a children's ballet for the town of Rybatskaya.

What Dasha did not know, was, somewhere in that town, a small girl's only dream left in life was to dance. The girl's name was Nina. When she danced at the tryouts for Swan Lake, Miss Bukovsky was so impressed by her natural ability she would have given Nina the lead role of Odette, had she not been so young and so petite. "She dances from the heart," she'd told those questioning her decision to put such a frail thing in her performance.

It meant the world to Nina to be chosen, yet there were times that the veil of grief swept over and seemed to paralyze her. Now, one week away from the festival, nine-year-old Nina no longer felt like dancing. She couldn't bear the thought of looking out to the audience and not seeing her mama. Her mama loved Nina's dancing. She would not be there to clap for Nina when it was all over.

"Please, Nina, dance for your Mama," Babushka begged. "She will be watching you from heaven."

"But what if I'm not able to dance when I get on the stage?"

"God will give you courage, Ninochka. You will see."

By week's end, Nina reluctantly gave in to Babushka's request, but only because she felt it wrong to say no to her grandmother. She pulled her white leotard and small tattered leather *cheshki,* ballet slippers, from the drawer they'd been cast into, and headed across the field to the town center for rehearsal. They met in the basement of the old clubhouse. The performance was to be held on the stage once all of the floor boards were shored up enough to hold the weight of a dozen prancing swans and one gallant prince.

Miss Bukovsky was surprised to see Nina, but glad she'd returned for the performance. "I've saved a spot for you, Nina. I was hoping you'd come back in time for our festival."

"I'm not sure I can dance anymore," Nina warned her.

"Nonsense. A true ballerina can always dance. You just need to warm up."

When The Dance of the Little Swans, began, Nina's feet didn't move as freely as they once had. She felt more like a big clumsy duck than a graceful little swan. She hoped her spirit would 'warm up' in time for the festival performance. Nina danced until the movements became familiar to her again and she could lose herself in the music. She danced until her legs were so wobbly she could barely stand, but she made it through to the end.

"I will see you all back here tomorrow for the dress rehearsal," Miss Bukovsky announced, and dismissed the class with a clap of her hands. When Nina stepped outside, her neighbor, Pasha, was waiting to walk her home.

"How did rehearsal go?"

Nina sighed. "I don't know if I can ever really dance again."

"Never dance again? Oh, Ninochka, of course you will dance again." He smiled at her serious frown. "Haven't you ever heard the story of 'The Tiny Dancer'?"

"No."

"Well, there was once a tiny duchess who was told she was too tiny to dance in the ballet. But she was so determined she danced in the meadows by herself all the time. As she grew older, no one ever asked her to dance at the royal dances because she was still so small she could barely be seen. But she kept dancing alone in the meadows.

"As time went on, she grew into a beautiful maiden. One day, she was dancing alone in the meadow and a handsome Duke rode by on his horse. He stopped and climbed down from his horse and watched the girl dance, but she did not see him because she always danced with her eyes closed.

"Suddenly, she sensed someone watching and opened her eyes. She was staring right into the eyes of the kind, handsome gentleman. He took her small hand and led her to the middle of the field and made a low bow toward her. Pasha bowed toward Nina. "'May I have this dance, Duchess Nina?'"

Nina giggled. "And who are you, Sir?"

"I am Duke Korotyshka, the smallest duke of the smallest kingdom in all of Russia. I have been searching throughout the land for a maiden small enough to dance with."

"Well, then, I suppose I can dance with you," Nina replied, with a curtsy.

Nina and Pasha bowed low toward one another and began a fancy waltz that they made up as they went, twirling and leaping in the middle of the field until they fell into a heap of laughter.

"You're right," Nina replied, maybe I can dance if I put my tiny mind to it."

Pasha laughed. "Good." And the two walked home.

~

On the evening of the festival, Nina huddled backstage with the other swans awaiting the cue for their piece. They were all to come out in a long line across the stage. Miss Bukovsky had borrowed some real feather costumes from the St. Petersburg Children's Ballet for the performance; fancier than anything these townsfolk had ever seen. Nina had barely pulled on her white feathered tutu when the opening curtain went up during the Swan Lake theme song. She closed her eyes, and let the music wash over her like a soothing balm. Her tight muscles began to relax.

As soon as Prince Siegfried danced away from his birthday celebration scene, Nina secured her white feathered head cap. In the following scene, Prince Siegfried discovered the Swan Princess on the pond. Nina heard the beginning notes to The Dance of the Little Swans. Clasping hands with the swans on her right and left, Nina pliéd her way across the stage in sync with the others. The quick tempo of the music helped perk her spirit. The lively notes sprang up from the stage floor, right through her small white slippers, and out to her limbs. She began prancing to the melody. But just as all the swans passed in front of the orchestra, Nina pranced too high, fell forward, and landed tail feathers up in the orchestra pit.

Nina didn't know if she should pop back up or just wait down in the pit until the show was over, then secretly crawl home in the dark to avoid the humiliation. The stage assistant jumped into the pit and shooed Nina out, telling her to go backstage.

Nina was beside herself with embarrassment and thought he'd said, "Go back on stage." She popped back up on the stage, not sure what she was supposed to do. After looking around, she realized she had popped right into the middle of the duet between Prince Siegfried and Princess Odette! She froze in place flapping her wings while the audience roared with laughter. She made a quick curtsy, then bravely fluttered her way off stage.

For Nina, the whole evening had been a disaster. She was too embarrassed to even look at Pasha as they began their trek home. Pasha glanced over at Nina and smiled.

"Stop smiling," she said. "There is nothing funny right now."

"Haven't you ever heard the story of Stumblelinka Ballerina?"

"No, and I don't want to hear one of your silly stories about a clumsy ballerina."

"Ah, but it's a true story about a young white swan who desperately wanted to be a ballerina. Most ballerinas want to be a swan, but this swan wanted to be a ballerina—yet she had these big clumsy feet that she was always tripping over."

"That's not funny," Nina replied.

"So one day she was waddling around in the forest when she heard a cry for help. She ran as fast as her big clumsy feet could carry her. She came upon a pond where she spotted a mama field mouse with a family of baby mice who had fallen out of a small canoe and were drowning. Stumblelinka did not know what to do. She knew how to swim, but her big webbed feet would cause such a big wake, it might swamp the struggling mice. So, she flew out to the mouse family and lowered herself down to the surface of the water; hovering over the mice while flapping her wings. Then, she put her big webbed feet out flat in first position as she had learned to do in ballet.

All of the mice babies grabbed ahold of Stumblelinka's feet, and climbed on board. Her feet were so big they were like a boat for the mice. Once the mama and all ten babies were safely aboard, Stumblelinka lifted off the surface of the pond and brought them all to safety. No one ever made fun of

Stumblelinka again. From then on everyone called her Stumblelinka Ballerina."

Nina tried her hardest not to smile. "That is not a true story," She protested.

"How do you know? You weren't there to see that it never happened."

Nina rolled her eyes. "I know it's not true because mice do not know how to row a canoe."

"You're right," Pasha agreed. "That's why the canoe tipped over."

After arriving home, Nina changed into her nightgown and went straight to bed. She prayed for her family before falling asleep; she prayed Mama, Papa, and Baby Tatiana had not really been watching her ballet performance from heaven. Her last thought was about Pasha's fairytale, Stumblelinka. She drifted off to sleep with a smile.

~

Nina loved the sea and preferred it over the family's elaborate home in St. Petersburg. Her Papa had been a proud Guardian of the Palace in St. Petersburg, and highly esteemed. Nina and her mama, with baby Tatiana, spent most of their summers by the sea in her Babushka's small cottage. This was now the only home she knew. All the family riches and wealth were swept away with the loss of her family. Nina now lived the life of a simple peasant with her dear Babushka. Babushka was Nina's only comfort, along with her memories. She tried daily to return to how her life was before, so as not to forget the family she loved. To do so, she closed her eyes, and listened to the sounds of the sea, remembering every detail of her past in the form of a ballet recital.

Each morning, Nina had greeted the dawn in ready position. Every sunrise had been a new spotlight that shone down on an empty stage awaiting her performance of the day.

She had started off in first position and headed toward the sea where an off-shore breeze beckoned to her young spirit and lured her to come explore along its rocky shore. After crossing the meadow, she had stopped to check up on the latest nests of eggs hidden in the brush by mama *chiyki, seagulls.* She had paused and observed the orderly march of the ants, already busy about their day's work of dismantling bits of straw that the chiyki had painstakingly built their nests with. Once the ants had their load secured on their tiny backs, they joined the others in the long procession home. Nina had pretended they were the accompanying orchestra and the bits of straw were their musical instruments. She joined in as their *Prima Donna,* lead ballerina, being careful not to crush them as she leapt her way up the sloping hillside.

Eventually, she had crested the top of the grassy dune with an arabesque and stared out to sea. She had stood there for a long time basking in the first rays of dawn, and breathing the fresh, salty air. She stood until her lungs were full and her soul revived, then she twirled down the grassy slopes to the seashore.

Once along the shoreline, the morning exploration had began; shiny sea shells, interesting rocks, iridescent bugs, new sea critters, fascinating birds flying overhead. When Nina had looked at something, she hadn't just looked, but saw everything right down to the finest detail, as though looking through a microscope. And in really seeing, her soul rejoiced, for nature was her proof that God existed, and He was everywhere present and in all things.

Each select rock or sea shell had been dropped into her apron pocket to bring home for Mama or Babushka, who showed great appreciation for the new findings. They were carefully added to various collections in jars or given a place of honor in the vegetable garden where Nina spent the cool hours of the morning weeding and watering everything her family counted on for food. Then, Nina made her way down to the barn where she'd begun her chores of feeding the family cow, Krem, their old plow horse, Nochka; Night; and their many chickens lined up for breakfast. It always ended with a graceful curtsy.

Mornings like that were fading memories. They now consisted of waking at dawn, dressing quickly, and walking alone to the small ancient church that sat above the shoreline of the sea. Albeit humble in size, it stood as a great beacon of hope for all of the fishermen who braved the stormy waters of the Baltic Sea. Its single weathered cupola pointed straight to heaven, and could be seen from afar when the sun shone upon it. When ships passed, passengers made the sign of the cross and prayed, many of them on their knees.

After arriving at the Chapel of St. Peter, Nina walked to the small cemetery out back, where she stood before three wooden crosses and wept. When she felt her heart would break, she drew away, went to the front and entered the church through the heavy wood door. Upon entering, she walked quietly to stand before the cross, and lit three candles. She waited patiently for consolation to come. If she waited long enough it eventually came, gently, softly, quietly. Then, she would return home to begin her chores.

The morning following the festival, the comfort did not come. Nina continued to wait, and nothing but more sorrow fell upon her young shoulders. In the midst of her heartache, the wood door creaked open. Pasha came quietly to where Nina was standing. He gently laid a hand on her shoulder. "Come, Ninochka, let's go home. Your grandmother is worried about you."

Twelve-year-old Pasha had known Nina since she was born and was like a brother to her. He'd always addressed her as Ninka, or more endearingly, Ninochka. Pasha sensed Nina's dependency on him, and did not take his role of guardianship lightly. He also took the role of caring for her babushka and his own mother equally seriously. He carried a hidden fear that one day he would not be able to hold up under the weight of all who depended on him.

Glancing once more at the icon of Jesus, Nina crossed herself, wiped her eyes with her scarf, and took Pasha's hand. The two walked silently out of the church and along the shoreline. Nina stooped down and picked up something in the sand. "Look, Pasha, it looks like a rabbit made of drift wood."

"Wow, it does," he admitted. "I could sand it down for you and make it nice and smooth and give it some eyes and a nose."

She handed it to Pasha. They cut across the meadow toward home as a gentle rain began to fall. "Pasha?" she inquired, "why did God take my family, but not me?"

Pasha looked at Nina, then toward the sea. "Why do you ask me questions that only God can answer?"

"Because, now that my Papa's gone, you're the wisest man I know," she replied, with sincerity.

Pasha stopped and turned to face Nina. "I'm not old enough to be the wisest. The wisest man I know is Father Nikolai. I don't know that he can help you with your question, but I do know he can answer the questions that matter most."

"I hoped to see him this morning. I wanted to ask him where Mama and Papa and Baby Tatiana are now. I wanted to ask him why God took them away from me. But Father Nikolai wasn't there."

"He's a busy man, Ninochka. Typhoid is still taking lives. All the families who lost family want to know the same things you do. Be patient and he will be back. Try again at Vespers. Father Nikolai is a good and wise man, just like your father was."

Nina's father, Alexander Maximovich Lashkov, was a good man. He had always provided well for his family, but without him, there was no way for Nina and Babushka to survive the harsh winter ahead on their own. Everyone in Rabatskaya struggled during winter, and only those with large gardens who were able to put up a pantry full of food fared well.

Once inside her home, Nina and Pasha sat at the

table beside the stove and bit into Babushka's warm apple piroshkies. Nina glanced at the empty chairs across from her. Babushka looked tired and worn as she stoked the small fire in the stove. For the first time, Nina wondered what would become of her if anything happened to her babushka. Until now, she'd never considered that those she loved would die before she grew up.

Pasha wiped the jam from his mouth and swallowed the last of his milk, which reminded him that it was milking time again. "Better get back to help Mama with the chores," he said, standing up. "Come by later if you like." He slipped out the door.

Nina curled up on the big chair beside the stove and slowly drifted off from the heat. She slept long and hard, making up for the nights she lay awake, unable to find sleep. A sudden knock at the door startled her out of the depths of her dreamless state. She arose in a stupor to open the door. "Father Nikolai," she said, in surprise. She held out her small hand. "Father, Bless."

Father Nikolai made the sign of the cross over her. "The blessing of the Lord, Ninochka."

Nina kissed his hand. "Come in," she offered, and held the door open.

The old Priest shuffled in, looking as weary as one would expect after visiting families in the midst of tragedy. He had not rested for days and still had families yet to visit. Babushka came from the back room and ambled slowly over to the Priest for a blessing. "Thank you for coming," she said. "Come, sit by the stove." She straightened the blanket and fluffed the tattered pillow before offering him their most comfortable seat. She went to the samovar, smelling of warm pitch from the burning pinecones inside its chamber, and poured him a cup of hot tea from the spigot. She and Nina sat down opposite him on an old worn couch.

The Priest looked at the two through weary eyes. Though he had spent the past weeks consoling his mournful flock, he looked at Nina as though his focus was solely on her. "Ninochka, how very sorry I am for you." He looked equally as sorrowful when he turned to Babushka. To her he said nothing, but his eyes expressed compassion. He returned his attention to Nina. "You are afraid, Ninochka?"

It did not seem unusual that Father Nikolai sensed her fear. He had a way of reading the hearts of his spiritual children, whom he knew so well. Nina nodded in response as tears trickled slowly down her cheeks. Knowing that he understood helped release some of her sorrow.

Father Nikolai crossed the room and sat on the couch beside her. He gently took both of her small hands in his own. "Ninochka," he spoke softly, "don't be afraid. Fear comes from realizing how small and weak we are, but courage comes from God. Take courage, Nina. God will help you."

Clara looked up from the notebook. "Do you have anymore?"

"I'm afraid you're a much faster reader than I am a writer."

Clara felt a pang of disappointment, which must have shown on her face.

"Don't worry; I will finish another chapter tonight."

"May I come again tomorrow?" Clara asked eagerly, surprising herself with such boldness.

"Of course you may. I enjoy the company."

Walking home, Clara thought about what Father Nikolai told Nina about courage.

She realized that, she, too, needed courage to endure the challenge of a new school where she knew no one, and no one seemed interested in knowing who she was. "Take courage," she whispered, "God will help me."

*

The second day of school was slightly better now that Clara had one new friend—even if she was an old lady. She was especially glad she had Tetushka's story to think about when one of her classmates whispered to the girl next to her in English class and they both looked over at her and laughed. Clara thought of Nina having everyone laugh at her when she fell into the orchestra pit. At least this wasn't that bad.

The lunch crowd for seventh grade girls was broken down to the pretty girls' table, the athletic girls' table, and the table of girls who wished they were one or the other. Only the eighth and ninth graders sat at coed tables. Clara preferred to avoid it all and retreated to the library.

Arriving home from school, Clara ran inside, dropped her school books on her bed, and announced she was going to Tetushka's house.

"Don't you want a snack first?" her mother asked.

"Tetushka will give me a snack with my tea," she replied.

"What about homework?" her mother called out when Clara was half-way out the front door.

"I only have to read a chapter in my History book tonight. Besides, I'm learning all about Russian history in '*Zorka*'. 'Bye." The door closed behind her.

Tetushka already had the tea water in the samovar heated and the tea cakes on small plates by the time Nina settled in by the fire. "I'm glad you've come to be my neighbor," Tetushka said. "I haven't had visitors for such a long time." She set the tea tray on the table in front of Nina and poured her tea. "Now then," she said, opening the book, "Let's see what happens next...

Winter 1908

As autumn pushed into winter, the morning trek to church became darker and colder. Early snows began to fly in November. Nina rummaged through her mama's dresser for warmer clothes. She pulled on thick wool socks and wrapped herself in her mama's fur cape, imagining her mama's arms wrapping around her. She tried to remember the sound of her voice and the way she would say, "My little Ninochka." The memories brought her comfort and sorrow, and she wasn't sure which was stronger.

Nina stayed warm all the way to church and back wrapped in the extra clothing. She was grateful to have something of her mother's, and knew that was part of the reason for the warmth. When she returned home, Babushka was sitting at the table with her shoulders hunched forward and her head down. A letter lay before her, unfolded.

'What's wrong?" Nina asked.

Her grandmother just shook her head.

"Who is the letter from?' Nina went to the table and glanced at the St. Petersburg return address. "Aunt Tonya wrote? What does she want?"

Babushka looked up with sad eyes. "She's coming for you Nina. She thinks it would be best if you went to live with her and Uncle Vasily in St. Petersburg."

Nina felt her knees grow weak. "St. Petersburg? But I don't want to live in St. Petersburg! I want to stay here with you and Pasha and our animals." She burst into tears. "I won't go! I can't go with her! Please don't make me go, Babushka."

Babushka was on the brink of tears herself. It was enough that the child lost both her parents and sister, but to take her from her Babushka was just unthinkable. "I don't want you to go, either, Ninochka, but I don't think Tonya will listen to me."

"When is she coming?" Nina asked.

"On the train, tomorrow."

"I won't be here when she comes. I will run away and she will never find me."

Babushka pulled Nina to her chest and held her close. "Maybe we can talk to her. We can try to reason with her." Babushka knew how stubborn her son-in-law's sister could be. Alexander had warned her about Tonya, but no one could stop her once he died. She swept in and took over the St. Petersburg estate and finances the minute the funeral was over. She wanted Nina too, but Nina begged to live with Babushka. Aunt Tonya had consented—for a short time, while she secured all of her brother's wealth in her own name. She would return in all of her pomp and frills, and try to take Alexander's most precious possession—his daughter.

Nina lay awake the entire night dreading the light of day. When it finally came, she heard the jingle of sleigh bells. Before she even saw the troika coming across the frozen steppe, she ran out the door and fled to Pasha's house. She burst through his front door without knocking. "She's here!" she yelled. "She's come for me! Don't let them take me!" she begged.

Pasha's mother knelt down and held Nina in a tight embrace. She'd met the aunt at the family's funeral and feared for Nina. "Oh Ninochka, we don't want her to take you either. Let me talk to her. I will tell her that we will take care of you."

Pasha came from the back room and looked as devastated as Nina. It felt as if someone were coming to take away his only sister. "Don't worry Nina, we will tell her you belong here."

When the troika arrived, a tall, proud woman wrapped in furs climbed down from the sleigh and started toward Nina's cottage. She planted a light kiss on Babushka's cheek as she strode through the front door. "Where is that niece of mine?" She peered around nervously, as though she were in a hurry to pack her up and leave.

"She's with the neighbors...but Tonya..."

Before Babushka could finish, Tonya was headed for Pasha's house. She rapped impatiently on the door.

"May I help you?" Liliya said, calmly.

"I've come for my niece; we have a train to catch."

Nina peered out from behind Pasha. "Hello Aunt Tonya," she said meekly.

"Well there you are. Come, Nina, we must be off if we're to catch the last train."

"Aunt Tonya I don't really want to go..."

"Don't be silly Nina, there's nothing here for you now that your mother..."

"Tonya," Liliya, cut in, "we would be very happy to watch over Nina if you will allow her to stay." Liliya knew from Nina's grandmother that Tonya was used to having her own way. Babushka had also indicated that Tonya had always been jealous that Nina's mother, Anna, had children and Tonya wasn't able to.

Tonya looked at Liliya, then glanced around the humble cottage. "Here? You want to keep Nina here, when she can have a proper upbringing in St. Petersburg?" She laughed, mockingly. "I'm sorry, but Nina will do much better in a culturally rich environment. She will have her own governess to take her to theaters and museums and all the other things lacking in village life. She will be introduced to everything a growing child should be introduced to." She looked at Nina. "I know the head of the St. Petersburg Dance Conservatory. You will be able to dance in the Nutcracker by Christmas."

"The Nu-nu-nutcracker?" Nina's bottom lip began to quiver. "Didn't you hear what happened when I danced in Swan Lake for the town festival? I fell into the orchestra pit and ruined the performance!" She burst into tears. "I c-c-can't dance!"

Pasha and Liliya both had to cover their mouths to hide their smiles. The whole community loved Nina and thought the festival a great success, even if it did turn into more of a comedy than a ballet. It was just what the town needed. Nina brought all the tension of difficult political times down to a night of joyful laughter.

"Never mind all that," Tonya retorted. "You didn't have the right instructors here. Now let's get your things and be off. I know this is what your father would have wanted for you."

"My daughter would want none of that for Nina," Babushka argued, standing at the front door. "Nina is perfectly happy here. Why take her away from us?"

"You have no idea how much more the child will benefit from what I have to offer." Tonya signaled to her driver who stood at ready with the horses. "Alexy, bring the horses around." She darted a harsh look toward Nina. "Go get your things, we'll miss the train." Tonya looked at what Nina was wearing, then recanted. "Never mind, just come as you are. I will need to buy you some decent things once we get there. She glanced around at all the eyes silently pleading with her to leave Nina behind. She turned and escorted Nina into the sleigh.

Everyone but Tonya was in tears as the sleigh set off. "Wait!" Pasha yelled. The horses were held up as Pasha ran to catch up and handed something to Nina. "Remember me," he said.

Nina took the small wood rabbit he had sanded down for her. She clutched it in her hand as the sleigh set off again across the white fields, disappearing into the horizon.

~

Nina was jolted awake as the train came to a

screeching halt. She peered around, trying to recall the reason for her sense of dread. St. Petersburg. It was no longer her home. Aunt Tonya gave Nina a brisk nudge to get her moving. "Let's be off, the sleigh should be waiting."

As the horse bells jingled through the snowy streets of St. Petersburg, Nina felt nervous anticipation; the familiarity of what was once home gave her an expected sense of joy, but the anxiety of knowing that those she'd loved were no longer there, left her empty. As the sleigh pulled up in front of the grand manor of her childhood, Nina's heart was bathed in memories. She stumbled through the front entrance in a daze. She peered around looking for things that had once brought her comfort; the wooden rocking horse in the foyer, her secret play area behind the couch where she kept her favorite dolls... all were gone.

The once simple, but elegant décor had been replaced with harsh, gaudy colors. Loud art hung from walls where family portraits used to welcome her. Her favorite small crystal chandelier in the living room was replaced by an imposing gold and brass fixture. The overall effect felt cold and unwelcoming. "Don't stand there gawking, child." Tonya directed her commands to a thin, nervous house maid. "Yulia, feed Nina some lunch, then take her to her room for a rest. We will be going out later to have her fitted for some decent clothing."

"Yes, Ma'am." She took Nina by the arm and escorted her away.

Awaking from a deep sleep, in the interim stage between wakefulness and dreaming, Nina peered around her former bedroom, expecting to see her baby sister in the bed beside her, and hear her mother humming softly through the house as she did when attending to her housework. Instead, she was quickly brought back by the voice of Aunt Tonya, "Get the girl up. We have a fitting at the tailor's."

The tailor shop was small and stuffy, crammed to the ceiling with bolts of fabrics of every texture and color. Aunt Tonya shot orders as Nina's limbs were pulled this way and that, and measurements were taken and written down by seamstresses. The whir of sewing-machines echoed from the back room. Nina wasn't asked which of the fabrics she liked as Tonya held up bolt after bolt and either approved or rejected them one by one. "I'd like these delivered to my home as soon as possible and put a rush on the ball gown."

For the first three nights in the strange house, Nina sobbed herself to sleep and could not be comforted even by the nervous little housemaid, who showed kindness to her only when Aunt Tonya was nowhere in sight. When it came to mealtimes, Nina was unable to eat more than two bites of her food without feeling that she would be ill if she swallowed any more. Despite the housemaid's pleadings and Aunt Tonya's unsympathetic demands, Nina continued to lose weight.

The night of the ball, Nina was brought before Aunt Tonya for approval, donning the most horrendous thing Nina had ever worn in her life. Her skinny frame was buried beneath layers of bright red ruffles and bows. The skirt of the gown billowed out so far she could barely walk without tripping. Her hair had been teased and tugged so much she had a headache and barely recognized herself when she glanced into a wall mirror. "You look fabulous," Aunt Tonya declared, dismissing any discomfort Nina was experiencing. "You will be presented as our daughter tonight at the ball."

Nina froze when she heard the words spill from her aunt's mouth. "Y-your daughter? But, you are not my mother, and Uncle Vasily is not my father."

"Well, from now on, we are your parents..."

Nina heard nothing past the word "parents." She fainted, and remained unconscious until she awoke hours later with a doctor at her bedside. He was in the middle of an argument with her aunt.

"What do you mean she shouldn't attend the ball?" Tonya replied. "Have you any idea how much this ball gown cost?"

"Beneath this ball gown, Madame, you have a very weak, malnutritioned child who is in no shape to go to a ball tonight."

Tonya left for the ball that night with only her husband and a fit of rage to accompany her.

In the days that followed, Nina did not recover but grew weaker. She was only able to eat when pressured to do so, but it resulted in an upset stomach every time. The doctor was summoned the following week when Nina did not respond to being shaken awake.

After a complete examination, the doctor stood back and gave his diagnosis: "The child is suffering from malnutrition, dehydration, and an acute case of homesickness."

"She's just a spoiled girl who thinks she can get what she wants by starving herself," her aunt replied. "She will eat again in time. I will not give in to this."

"I'm afraid you have used all the time she had to spare. She is nothing but skin and bones. This child either goes home now, or you will have a dead child on your hands to answer for."

~

After Nina's departure from Rabatskaya, Pasha, Liliya, and Babushka asked Father Nikolai for special prayers regarding Nina. Father Nikolai was solemn. He knew Nina's heart. Although she might get a better education in St. Petersburg, her spirit would suffer greatly. He also knew Tonya had no regard for Nina's soul.

November came and went, and no word from St. Petersburg. Babushka made the painful walk to church with Pasha and Liliya every Sunday to ask for prayers for Nina and to light a candle for her. Father Nikolai continued to mention her name during the Divine Liturgies and told Babushka not to lose hope, for God was with Nina and would not forsake her. Babushka always left with a renewed sense of hope to help carry her through the following week.

In early December, the three were slowly treading their way home in the snow, making allowances for Babushka's bad leg when they heard a faint jingling of bells far away. Pasha stopped in his tracks. The ringing became clearer and louder until, in the distance, a dark silhouette could be seen moving across the steppe. Pasha did not wait for it to come any closer, but took off through the frozen fields to meet the approaching sleigh.

As it drew near, Pasha's heart began to sink, as he could make out only two people in the sleigh, that of the driver and one passenger. Surely if it were Nina, she would be escorted by an adult. But as the sleigh approached, he heard his name.

"Pasha!" A small form jumped from the sleigh and ran straight for him.

"Nina!" he called back. "Nina!" The two ran right into each other's arms and spun in circles, hugging until the two women had a chance to catch up to them. Babushka was sobbing "Nina" over and over in an engulfing embrace. "What happened? Where's Tonya? How did you get home?"

All four climbed into the sleigh together. Beneath warm fur blankets, Nina re-capped the story for them on the way home:

"When we got to St. Petersburg, they brought me to our old house, but it no longer looked like our house. It looked like a palace inside with big brass chandeliers hanging from the ceilings and gold statues everywhere, but I wasn't allowed to touch anything. There was nowhere to run or play; no fields or animals or creeks nearby—just buildings, noise, and people everywhere.

"I was so homesick I couldn't stop crying. I kept asking to go home but Aunt Tonya just said I was spoiled and wasn't thankful for all of my beautiful new things. She began leaving me with her housemaid all the time, who was at least nicer than Aunt Tonya. But every night I would pray for God to take me back home.

"Aunt Tonya took me to a dressmaker and had

these fancy dresses made for me that I could barely walk in. They had big matching ribbons and bows and I felt very silly in them and looked ridiculous. Then, she tried to take me to a fancy ball to introduce everyone to me. She planned to tell everyone that I was their daughter. Uncle Vasily told me that God sent me to them because they couldn't have a child of their own.

"I got so sick after that they had the doctor come, and told him to make me eat. He told her I was homesick and the only cure was to send me back home or I might starve to death. Finally, they gave up and sent Miss Yulia to the train with me. She rode with me on the train from St. Petersburg, then hired me a sleigh and driver and sent me on alone. And now," Nina sighed deeply, looking at the three she loved so dearly, "I am home."

That night, both Nina and Babushka knelt before the icon of Christ and thanked Him for bringing her safely home. Nina slept well for the first time in over a month.

Home Again

It was heaven for Nina to wake up in her own bed again, beside Babushka. The first thing she did when she awoke was visit the horses. Nina could not get enough of the animals and the outdoors again. She went for snow walks every chance she got.

Trudging along the frozen ground on her way to church, Nina left a trail of crumbs from her warm biscuits for the birds. Becoming accustomed to this, the birds often waited in ambush for her in various shrubs and bushes that lined her path. Nina began to recognize some of her repeat customers. Her favorite was a tiny black and white *lastoshki*, sparrow, who reappeared every time. To help encourage him, Nina held out a big crumb in the palm of her hand, and called to him; *"Ede suda malen kaya ptichka,"* come here little bird.

It became apparent that he understood Nina's

good intentions, for within two weeks of her continued coaxing, he finally swept over, lighted on her hand for a fleeting second, and whisked away with the huge crumb in his tiny beak. This single act of bravery inspired his entire flock to follow suit. It wasn't long before Nina was followed by small black and white birds all the way to church, eagerly waiting their turn to snatch up her warm crumbs. The most surprising of all, was a small red fox who often crept from his den to receive the gifts his young benefactress often brought for him. Nina was so touched that these shy wild creatures trusted her; she never spoke of it to anyone.

Keeping a protective watch over his young wandering friend, Pasha came silently upon such scenes with his own eyes. Sensing the sacredness behind it, he'd retreat, and never spoke of it as well, even to Nina. He had learned from Father Nikolai that some souls are so gentle, even the animals trust them. Father. Nikolai also warned that some things in life are better left to ponder than to be spoken aloud. He had said, "Even the Mother of God, when observing the things that touched her soul, did not speak of them, but 'pondered them in her heart.' To speak of such things is to diminish them."

~

During The Nativity, all of Rybatskaya flocked to St. Peter's as often as they could. A heavy snowfall had just covered the steppe, making the trip long and difficult. Some were fortunate enough to make the trek in horse-drawn troikas or sleighs.

Nina loved the Nativity season. She loved the fresh crisp air filled with falling white flakes, and the sound of tinkling bells as horses escorted villagers from place to place.

One especially beautiful morning, the sun broke through the clouds and lit up the fields like sparkling crystal. Nina stepped through the doors of St. Peter's, and was enveloped by more rays of sunlight streaming through the swirling incense. Clouds of heaven, Nina called it. She slowly made her way to the candle stand to light her candles. Soothing flames flickered through deep red glass jars. In this place, Nina's soul drew as near as possible to God, and heaven, and to the family she had lost. Where that was, she wasn't sure, but when she was here, she felt it was near.

Starting back home, Nina ran to catch up with Pasha, her long dark hair flying behind her. Pasha was strides ahead of her talking to a gentleman in a troika about his horses. The three horses were fully decorated with bells and ribbons against their deep, black velvet coats. The middle horse shook his magnificent head with impatience, sending peals of ringing bells into the frozen air. Nina was thrilled by this and reached into her jacket pocket to reward the gelding for his display of majesty with a cube of sugar.

"That's a bit like giving gold to a beggar," the horses master commented. "He'll be your friend for life now."

The sugar cube was one of the last from a box of sugar her father had given to Nina as a gift on her ninth birthday. She'd savored them for months, and shared with only those she felt deserving, such as hard-working horses.

The man and his horses moved on and Pasha turned to Nina with a gleam in his eye.

"What are you up to Pasha—what did that man say to you?"

Pasha smiled down at Nina. "I have a plan for us. I think I have of a way to make a living for both of our families, and perhaps even make enough extra to buy ourselves a fancy troika one day."

Nina's bright green eyes lit up. "Really? Tell me!" Nina loved the way Pasha always included her in his plans as though they were brother and sister. It gave her heart such courage to feel that she would not be left alone in the world without a friend, should anything happen to Babushka.

Pasha took a seat on a fallen log to explain the plan to Nina, who was so winded from running; she lay in the snow in the form of a snow angel and glanced over with anticipation.

"Well," he began, "Mr. Bardzecki has that beautiful troika he might be willing to sell or trade."

"Who has enough of anything to get a troika? We will all be lucky to survive the winter. Troikas are for rich and fancy people, not poor *muzhiks,* peasants, like us. Besides, you need three horses to pull a troika."

"Well, your mare, Nochka, is going to foal in spring, right?"

"Yes."

"And my stallion, Zakhar, is the sire, true?"

"Yes, but we couldn't make much money taking poor people around in a troika. Who could afford to pay us?"

"No, Nina, we would only offer rides in the

winter. In spring and summer, we would train the foal to plow gardens and he could work for hire in the town when people need their gardens plowed. We could work for trade or for money. If we plowed for the fishermen, we could trade for fresh fish."

"But what if people are harsh with him, I couldn't bear that."

Pasha glanced down at Nina with tenderness. "Ninka, no one is going to be harsh to our foal because we will be the ones leading him. They will hire us as a team. We will go wherever he goes."

A team. She, Pasha, and the foal would be a team. Her smile was her reply of acceptance in the new plan.

"Let's get home, it's freezing out here." Pasha jumped up, shook off the snow, and extended his hand to Nina, pulling her up with one small tug. "We will make a good team—but first you need to get some meat on your bones if you're to push a big draft horse around and get him to mind you."

"I will bribe him with sugar," she joked.

"Then you will spoil him, and he'll have no teeth left!"

Bringing in Christmas

Nina wandered along the snow-covered roads looking for pretty greens with red berries to make some festive winter decorations. She would make enough to add some cheer to her own cottage, and Pasha's cottage, but especially, to help decorate the church for the Nativity. Nina loved finding beautiful things that grew outdoors to bring inside. It was her way of showing her appreciation to The One who made such wonders. She had an eye for arranging beauty out of God's bounty.

The majority of Rybatskaya was made up of rocky shores, and fields and meadows inland. Greenery such as trees and boughs were only found on the outskirts of town at the edge of the forests. Nina thought perhaps she could ride Nochka out to the edge of the woods but it was quite a long way to go in the snow. Trudging along the snowy lane, Nina spotted a large green mountain ash shrub covered with bright red berries. The only drawback was they bordered a fence that belonged to old Zlata Frinovskii, who was dubbed The Town Hag.

Nina sidled up alongside the street side of the fence and cautiously began snapping off the berry-clad boughs that hung down in arms reach. Just as she was snapping her last bough, a mass of wild black hair on a shriveled face popped over the top of the fence. A pair of wild eyes flashed at Nina, who froze like a statue. "How dare you steal my boughs!" she shrieked. "I'll have you arrested, you little scoundrel!" She grabbed for Nina's arm with her bony claws, but got a handful of thistle that was mixed in with the boughs. A horrific screech rang out as the spindly claw quickly retreated to the other side of the fence, and Nina just as quickly dropped her armload of boughs on the ground and high-tailed it down the lane as fast as her shaky legs could carry her! She didn't slow down until she flew right into Pasha as he was rounding the side of the barn.

"Whoa, Ninochka!" He swung her small frame around and steadied her. Once he had her by the shoulders, he held her still until she could catch her breath "What is it? What's happened?"

"It's... it's Zlata Frinovskii! She... she... caught me stealing her boughs...."

"You were stealing them?" Pasha asked, in surprise.

"I wanted to make wreathes for the church. They were on the outside of her fence."

"Oh, Ninka," he laughed, "stealing for the church, were you?"

"Is it a sin when it's on the other side of the fence?" she asked, still breathless.

Pasha smiled down at her. "That's something you'll have to take up with Father Nikolai, but it may not be so bad that it's on the other side of the fence." He draped his arm around Nina's shoulder. "Come on, I know where we can get some nice boughs for your wreathes. We're going to have to hitch up the old sleigh to Zakhar to do it."

"Really? Did you fix the sleigh?" Nina loved riding in the horse-drawn sleigh through the snow, but one of the runners had come loose the past winter and brought an end to the sleigh rides.

"I fixed it enough to get us through one trip to the forest, and hopefully a few rides to church for the Nativity Fast so your Babushka won't have to walk." He led Nina out to the barn where the old sled was stored. "I'll hitch up the sleigh if you'll pack us some biscuits for the trip."

~

Saturday night vigil was followed by confession. Nina tried to spread her confessions out to every other Saturday, so as not to look like such a bad sinner, but somehow she ended up going every week. Her conscience was sensitive and she felt the weight of carrying too much guilt around for too long. This week in particular she knew she needed to repent of the incident with Zlata Frinovskii.

She stood in the candlelit darkness facing the icon of Christ while Fr. Nikolai stood at her side as she spilled her heart out to the Lord. "I stole from old Mrs. Frinovskii. But I only wanted a few boughs for the church wreaths and they were on the outside of her fence. She screamed her head off at me like an old witch and I'm sorry to say that I think I hate her."

Father Nikolai had Nina kneel while he placed his stole on her head. He prayed that she not take her sins lightly but that God forgive her for what she had confessed, and made the sign of the cross over her.

Nina stood back up and waited. The chapel went completely still and Fr. Nikolai remained silent for what felt like a very long time. Nina would have begun to worry except that she was used to this awkward silence following her confessions. She knew that Fr. Nikolai prayed and weighed his every thought before he spoke.

"Ninochka," he began, "regarding Zlata Frinovskii, it was wrong for you not to ask before picking the boughs, but the thoughts you have toward this poor old woman are more troubling than taking the boughs." Nina waited while he formed his thoughts further. "When we think hateful thoughts toward others, it is like giving them blows. They are hurt by our thoughts as though we were hitting them. We cannot know the pain that others bear that cause them to harbor such anger, only God knows this. But the only way we can help them is by praying for them and having kind thoughts toward them. Our thoughts are very powerful. They can carry as much weight as our physical actions. Do you understand what I am telling you, Ninochka?"

"Yes, but she is a very scary lady to have kind thoughts toward. All the kids at school say she's a witch."

"And what makes them think she is a witch?"

"Well, she looks like one. Her hair is all black and sticking out everywhere. And she dresses in old rags and wears boots with pointed toes. And she lives in an old shack like witches usually do."

Father Nikolai stroked his long, white beard for a moment. "Let me read you something I've just read by Archpriest John Iliytch Sergieff." He reached for a book on the cantor stand and held a candle over the page as he read:

"'Do not forget yourself in looking upon the beauty of the human face, but look upon the soul; do not look upon the man's garment but look upon him who is clothed in it. Do not admire the magnificence of the mansion, but look upon the dweller who lives in it and what he is—otherwise you will offend the image of God in man, will dishonor the King by worshipping His servant and not rendering unto Him even the least of the honor due Him.'"

"Now, this reading is about loving someone for their outward beauty and forgetting to look at the soul inside that reflects the image of their Maker. But we can also dishonor God by hating someone for being outwardly unlovely, without ever looking to see the image of God inside of them."

"But she's really mean inside, too."

"Maybe underneath that outward unpleasantness there's someone inside worth knowing. Pray for Zlata Frinovskii. See if somehow you can't look further to see who's really inside. Perhaps by your kindness you can help her to bear whatever burden has caused her such pain. And let it remind you, too, not to become bitter towards life's hardships. They are sent to us for a reason and for our good."

Walking home in the dark of night, Nina contemplated what Father Nikolai had said. With each quiet step she took through the snow, she considered what fate may have caused such pain.

"I think this is a good place to stop reading today," Tetushka said, following a yawn. "Next time we will find out why this poor woman has such great pain in her life that would cause such anger."

"If I finish my homework early tonight, could I come hear a little more?"

"Oh, I would like that, but I have church tonight."

"Church? At night?" Clara had never heard of night church before.

"Yes, this is the Nativity fast, just like in the story. We attend more church services during the Nativity season to prepare for the birth of Christ."

Clara was curious. "How do you do that?"

"We try to pray a little more, and help others in need. We have a little less that others may have more—either of our time, or help, or resources."

"Where is your church, Tetushka?"

"It's about twenty miles from here. A small community of Russians settled here during the time of the Bolshevik revolution to avoid persecution. I was among them. I was just a young woman then, barely twenty years old. We brought our own Priest and built a small church. Nearly all of the original immigrants have passed on now..." Tetushka's voice trailed off. "There are more young families now," she added on a lighter note. "But we still have some beautiful old icons and relics that were brought with us from Russia. I'll have to take you sometime."

"I would like that."

"Good. We will ask your mama sometime. For now, I will light a candle for you and your family."

On her way home, Father Nikolai's words resonated with Clara. She began to realize what kind of pain in her own life was making her feel so angry. Leaving everyone and everything she'd ever known behind and having to start all over on her own in this strange town. It helped to know there was a reason for the way she felt. And her problems didn't seem quite so big compared to Nina's.

~

The following week, Clara began to ride the school bus. She doodled in her school binder to appear occupied while sitting alone, as the other students chattered away with one another. Thursday afternoon there were no empty seats available except one—next to a girl she'd seen in the library. She always sat alone—the only one besides herself that no one seemed to make an effort to include in anything. Clara approached the girl's seat.

"May I sit here?" Clara asked.

The girl looked up. She was thin and pale, and her wavy dark hair was somewhat disheveled. But she had kind eyes. "Uh, sure." She replied, and slid over to make room.

"I'm Clara."

The girl glanced over shyly. "Annie," she whispered, as though she were embarrassed to say her own name.

"I just moved here," Clara informed her. "Have you lived here long?"

"About four months."

"Do you have a farm?" Everyone but Clara seemed to have a farm.

"No. I live with my aunt above the café."

"Ruby's?" Clara asked. After all, there was only one café in town.

"Yes. That's our café."

Clara nodded. "I've seen you in the library during lunch. Do you like to read?"

"I love books," she nodded.

The bus screeched to a stop in front of the cemetery. "Me too." It made Clara wonder if Annie would like the kind of story she was reading at Tetushka's house.

"There's my house," Clara said, nodding across the street. "Well, see you tomorrow... Annie."

"Yeah. Maybe I'll see you in the library." She gave Clara a faint smile.

Clara felt lighter as she stepped off the bus. Sadness sure can weigh a person down, she thought. She thought of Tetushka and the story. Clara hadn't been to visit Tetushka all week due to a science project she had to work on. She could hardly wait to see what happened next with Nina and mean old Zlata the Witch. This time, Clara told her mom that she promised to finish her science report that night if she could go straight to Tetushka's before coming home. Her mom consented—as long as she only stayed one hour.

When Nina arrived, the room was filled with the scent of warm butter and sugar. Tetushka brought out a plate of what she called "soldier cookies." Nina had never tasted anything so wonderful; nuts and shortbread and powdered sugar.

"I was hoping you'd come. I missed you this week."

"I've been dying to know what happens with Nina and mean old Zlata!"

"Well, let's find out...." Tetushka handed the next chapter to Clara, who settled back in her seat after grabbing another soldier cookie.

Nina crept up the rickety front steps of Zlata's run down cottage. She was tempted to just drop her basket of apple piroshky at the door and run. Perhaps making a social visit to the woman who had nearly clawed her head off was not such a good idea. But ever since talking with Father Nikolai, she could not get his words out of her mind. She also remembered what he'd said about courage. She prayed for courage and took another step to the front door.

Nina knocked lightly, half hoping Zlata was not home. A pair of shuffling feet inched their way to the door, then it creaked open and two dark beady eyes peered through the sliver. "You again? Come to steal from me again, have you?"

"No, Ma'am... I..." She held the basket of warm pastries out to where it could be seen from the sliver in the door. The scent of fresh baked apple filling wafted inside along with the cold wind. "I brought you some of my Babushka's apple piroshky."

Zlata Frinovskii Sokolova inched the door open just far enough to get a good look at what she was being offered. "What's it for?" she demanded. Her wild black hair stuck out in every direction, looking every bit the witch she was accused of being.

"Because it's Christmas."

Zlata cocked her head to one side to hear better. "Christmas, you say?"

"Yes, the Nativity of Baby Jesus is only three days from now."

"Well, don't just stand there filling my house with cold air then, come inside if you've got something to give me."

Nina tapped the snow from her boots and stepped inside, passing the basket to Zlata on her way through the door.

"Fix yourself a seat there by the stove." She gestured to the small wooden stool that sat beside an old black stove. Zlata's home was small, but tidy. To Nina's delight, she was quickly surrounded by three furry cats who kept her company as she waited for Zlata to set the basket down and take a seat herself. After much shuffling, she finally relaxed on a stool at the table, then reached for the biggest piroshky and bit into it, closing her eyes with pleasure.

Nina looked around for signs of others who might live with the old woman. She spotted one small photo of a girl beside an icon of Jesus in the corner where a candle burned. "Do you have children?" Nina asked.

Zlata pointed to the photo. "A daughter. I had one daughter."

"Where is she now?" Nina replied.

Zlata looked out the window. "She went away."

A wave of sadness filled Zlata's eyes and Nina wished she hadn't asked about the girl in the photo.

"She was my life," Zlata whispered. "But she's gone now."

"Where did she go?"

"She ran off with a man not deserving of her. Broke my heart. I've not seen her nor heard from her for over five years."

Nina saw a tear on Zlata's cheek. "Do you want to come to church with me for Christmas day?"

Zlata shook her head. "I used to go... with Natalia."

Nina looked around the small, dreary room. There must be something that could be done. "Would you like me to bring you a New Year's tree? I could help you decorate it."

Zlata looked up. A faint spark flickered in her eye. "A tree? It's been a long time since I had a tree. I used to have the prettiest tree in Rabatskaya. Natalia and I made all of our decorations ourselves. She was so proud...." She couldn't finish, but looked sadly away.

"Do you still have them?"

Zlata nodded.

"May I see them?" Nina so wanted to see what she and her daughter had made that once made this old woman so happy, and this room the prettiest in the town.

Zlata gave Nina a puzzled expression. "You're a queer one, aren't you?" She cocked her head in thought. "I guess I'd have to remember where I put them if I'm to show them to you."

"I have an idea," Nina spoke up. "I will go cut you a tree while you try and find your decorations, then we can meet back here and decorate your tree together."

"Well, just so long as you don't go cutting down any of my own trees out front!" A hint of her old witchy tone was added in but Nina wasn't afraid this time. There was a flicker of light in Zlata's cloudy old eyes that told Nina this woman wasn't as mean and scary as she'd wanted Nina to believe.

"I promise I won't. I'll get Pasha to go to the woods with me. We can have Zakhar pull the tree on the sled to your house." Nina was so excited she jumped up quickly and ran for the door, her wet boots leaving a trail of snow behind. "I'll be back soon!" she yelled on her way out, not even waiting for an answer. She didn't want Zlata to have the chance to say "No."

~

By the time Nina and Pasha arrived with the tree, Zlata had all of her handmade ornaments displayed and waiting on her dining table. Pasha left Nina with Zlata to decorate and rode away on Zakhar, pulling the empty sled home behind him.

Nina looked at each of the decorations with awe. They were delicately hand painted winter scenes on wooden eggs, and were absolutely beautiful. "Did you really paint these yourself, Zlata?" she asked.

"I did," she replied. "I once sold my eggs in a small shop in town every winter. They sold quite well."

"Why do you not sell them any longer?"

Zlata got a faraway look in her eye. "I guess I just lost heart...." Her voice drifted off and she never finished her sentence. "At any rate, we have enough to cover that pretty tree with, so let's get started."

Clara paused from reading and reached for another cookie.

"My grandmother's favorite recipe," Tetushka told Clara.

The fact that she was on her third cookie confirmed that she approved. "Maybe I could learn to make these sometime?" she half hinted, half questioned.

"I'd be happy to teach you," Tetushka replied. "We'll make some for your family for Christmas—if we don't eat them all ourselves first. They are hard to resist straight from the oven."

Clara laughed, while taking another bite.

"You seem happier today," Tetushka told her.

Clara caught herself smiling. "Yes. I do feel better. I-I met a new friend today," she said quietly.

Tetushka nodded. "What is your friend's name?"

"Annie. She lives one bus stop past mine—above the café with her aunt."

"How nice for you," Tetushka replied. "A good friend can make a great difference in one's life."

~

When Clara went to get on the bus Friday morning, Annie had saved the seat next to her for Clara. It was the last day of school before Christmas break began. Clara was hoping to have someone to spend time with over the two-week break. She so wanted to ask, but was afraid she'd appear too forward; after all, they'd just met the day before. Clara suddenly remembered the word *courage*, from *Zorka*, and took a deep breath. "My mom said it would be alright to invite someone over to go sledding after school today—if you'd like to come."

Annie looked almost shocked, and Clara was worried that perhaps she shouldn't have been so bold after all.

"Really? Come to your house?" Annie said it as though maybe she'd heard her wrong.

"I mean, if you aren't already busy...." Clara tried to give her an out just in case she needed one.

Annie actually laughed. "You're the first person to ever invite me to do anything. I would love to come. I can call my aunt from school and let her know."

Clara smiled with relief. "That would be great."

~

Annie got off at Clara's stop that afternoon. Walking to the house, Clara noticed that Annie's hip rotated slightly forward when she walked. She hoped she'd be okay for sledding.

Once on the snow, Annie's hip didn't seem to pose a problem. The two girls had a great time sledding down the slope in Clara's back pasture. They made a sled jump that landed them in a pile of soft snow. They went inside when they could no longer feel their hands and feet. After drinking hot cocoa piled with marshmallows, they went into Clara's bedroom where Clara showed Annie the bulletin board she'd made of her former life and friends. "It was really hard for me to move here," she told Annie.

"It's been hard for me too," Annie replied. "You're really the first friend I've met since I came to live with my aunt." Annie looked suddenly distant. She slowly turned her gaze back to Clara. "There was an accident," she said.

Clara felt a lump in her throat, but said nothing.

"My mom and dad...." She shook her head.

Clara felt her eyes sting, and she nodded slowly.

"I was asleep in the backseat. I hurt my leg and hip, but that's all."

Clara nodded again. She thought of Nina who had also lost both her parents. She wondered again if Annie might like to hear the story she'd been reading—maybe it would help Annie to know someone else who went through such a tragedy. "I need to tell you something...." Clara told Annie all about Tetushka and the story that she was reading at her house.

An hour later the two girls arrived together on Tetushka's front porch with a wreath they had made from some pine boughs.

"How lovely! And you've brought a little friend. Come inside. Shall we have some tea?"

"We were hoping we could both read *Zorka* today—if you're feeling up to visitors?"

"Ah, today would be a very good day for *Zorka*. Annie can start at the beginning, and you can read ahead, Clara. You were just getting to Nina's Christmas."

Tetushka got Annie all set up on the couch by the fire with the first chapter, while Clara eagerly dove into the chapter on Christmas....

Christmas Eve

After Christmas Eve vigil, there was a knock at the door. Nina came from the back room and was surprised to see Zlata standing in the entrance. She had walked in the cold and dark to come visit. "Come in, come in," Babushka urged and escorted her to the seat by the stove.

Zlata was carrying a package all wrapped in beautiful, shiny paper. As Zlata walked past Babushka she held the gift out to Nina. "This is for you," she said, and pushed the package into her hands. Nina didn't know what to say. She stood and marveled at the shimmering paper as if that alone was a gift in itself.

"Open it," Zlata urged.

She opened it slowly, hoping to keep the paper from ripping so she could use it again for something special.

When the paper lay open, Nina gently lifted the garment and watched as a beautiful Christmas dress unfolded before her eyes. It was red velvet with black and green velvet ribbon sewn in fine detail around the hem and sleeves. It was the most exquisite dress she had ever seen.

"I made it myself," Zlata said. "It was for Natalia when she was your size. She only wore it for a short time before she outgrew it, but it was her favorite dress. I'd like you to have it."

"Oh, Zlata," Nina whispered. How could Zlata have known that Nina had just outgrown the last dress her mother had made for her? It broke her heart. Zlata would never know how much her gift meant to Nina. A tear ran down Nina's cheek as she crossed the room and placed a gentle kiss on Zlata's bony white face, while wrapping her arms around the spindly old woman. "It's just beautiful," she whispered.

"Enough of that," she barked, but did nothing to push her away. "Now go try it on—I haven't got all night."

Nina turned away but caught Zlata wiping a tear from her own cloudy eyes.

"Oh Zlata, please come with us to church for the Nativity Feast tomorrow," Nina pleaded.

"Oh, yes," Babushka added, "You must. And you must stay with us tonight—it's far too cold and dark for you to go back home alone tonight. We are just sitting down to a warm supper and have plenty to share."

"Well...." Zlata glanced at the fish pie, *pirog*, cooling on the stove. "If you're sure."

Christmas morning the women were escorted to church in a horse-drawn sleigh, as promised by Pasha. Pasha and Nina sat in front, and Zlata,

Babushka, and Liliya sat in the backseat huddled under a fur blanket.

Nina closed her eyes and sighed deeply at the melodious ringing and jingle of the bells as Zakhar moved along through the fresh fallen snow. Steam rose from the horse's back as his warm sweat mingled with the freezing air, making a misty white path for the sleigh to follow.

Old Zakhar pranced slowly. It helped that there were a few other horses along the way to show off for; his head and gait picked up each time he saw them.

The church was beautifully decorated with the fresh boughs and wreathes that Nina and Pasha had brought in from the forest. The scent of pine mingling with the incense smelled like Christmas.

There was something so mystical about the birth of Jesus. The remembrance of Almighty God coming to earth as a humble baby among animals and shepherds helped Nina to better receive Him, being a child herself.

~

"Today He who holds the whole creation in His hand is born of a virgin.

"He whose essence none can touch is bound in swaddling-clothes as a mortal man.

"God who in the beginning fashioned the heavens lies in a manger.

"He who rained manna on his people in the wilderness is fed from his mother's breast.

"The Bridegroom of the church summons the wise men.

"The Son of the Virgin accepts their gifts."

Many of the children went staring, carrying handmade stars on tall wooden poles, and sang Christmas hymns from house to house on Christmas day, receiving gifts and candy from each house they visited.

The words to David's Psalm 116 rang through Nina's mind all the way home;

"What shall I render to the Lord for all his goodness to me?

"I will take up the cup of salvation and call on the name of the Lord."

The Feast Day of St. Nina
January 1909

N ina was up at dawn preparing a honey cake for her saint's name day. Traditionally, one would prepare a feast to share with others on their saint's feast day. Without her mother to help, the best Nina could offer was her honey cake. Babies in Russia are baptized with the name of a saint given by their parents or priest. Nina loved the story of the saint whose name she bore.

Every January 27th the church commemorated St. Nina. This time her name day fell on a Sunday. Nina wore Zlata's dress and was happy to see Zlata arrive at church that morning to share her special day.

After the reading of the Gospel, Father Nikolai came forward to deliver his homily. Nina loved this part of the service the most. Everyone was allowed to sit on the floor and listen to a story of a saint or a Bible teaching. Nina tucked her feet under the hem of her soft velvet dress and scooted into a comfortable position in anticipation of the story of St. Nina.

"Today," Father Nikolai began, "the church honors St. Nina of Georgia. Nina was the niece of the Jerusalem Patriarch Juvenal. From early childhood, she loved God with all her heart and deeply pitied those who did not believe in Him. Her father Zebulon, of Cappadocia, left for a hermitage and her mother became a deaconess, after which St. Nina was given to a pious nun for her education. The nun frequently told Nina of Georgia when it was yet a pagan country. This instilled in Nina a strong desire to visit this country and to share with its people the light of the Gospels.

"When the Lord opened a path to her, the young Nina indeed went to Georgia, with a cross made of grapevines, where she quickly gained the love of the people. She baptized Mirian, the Tsar of Georgia, his wife Nana and their son, Bakar, who then aided Nina in her missionary efforts zealously.

In the course of her life, St. Nina traveled throughout Georgia, bringing its people to the Christian faith, all during the time when the Emperor Diocletian was fearfully persecuting Christians. Nina was the only one of thirty-nine nuns with whom she traveled to escape martyrdom. Hearing of the power of her prayers, many of the sick began to come to her. The

Bishop and priests of Constantinople were summoned, and the first church was built in Georgia, dedicated to the Apostles. Slowly, almost all of Georgia became Christian.

"St. Nina, desiring neither honor nor fame, withdrew to a mountain and there, in solitude, thanked God for the conversion of the pagans to Christianity. After several years she gave up her solitude and went to Kahetia where she converted the Tsarina Sofia to Christianity. She rested from her many labors and entered into peace in the Lord in the year 335. On the place of her death, the Tsar Marian erected a church in honor of the great martyr George, a distant relative of St. Nina. Her grave is in a church in Samtavro. May we honor her memory this day."

After the Eucharist, everyone gathered in the basement of the church where steaming bowls and plates of food were set out on bright table cloths for the feast. After reciting the Lord's Prayer and asking the Father's blessing, Father Nikolai made a special announcement. "We are honored to have our own Nina Komonovsky among us today to celebrate the Feast of St. Nina with. God grant you many years!"

With Nina turning crimson red, the entire church body burst into many rounds of the traditional song, sung to one on their name day, "God Grant You Many Years."

As a gift, Father Nikolai presented Nina with her very own icon of St. Nina that had been hand painted by a nun at a woman's monastery. Nina was so touched to have her own saint's icon that she carried it with her all day, holding it tightly on her lap even during the feast. When others came to admire it, she held it up for them, but was reluctant to let anyone else hold it for fear she might lose it, as she had with so many other things in her life.

That night before bed, Nina placed her icon of St. Nina on a small table in the east corner of the room that she and Babushka shared. She said a prayer asking that St. Nina, being so close to God in heaven, would ask Him to greet her mama, papa, and baby sister for her. She fell asleep in hopes that God was doing so even as she slept.

~

Tetushka paused from her translation and poured more tea for the girls. "Are you enjoying the story?" she asked Annie.

When Annie looked up, she had tears in her eyes. "Very much," she whispered, "thank you."

Babushka smiled gently, "Good girl." She turned and handed more pages to Clara. "Part Two will jump ahead a few years now to where Nina is twelve years-old—the same age as you two."

Part ll

Early Spring
1911

Nina awoke from a loud whinny down at the barn. It was followed by a quiet nicker. She threw off her covers and ran to the barn. Her mare, Nochka, lay in a cold sweat on the damp straw, breathing heavily.

The early rays of light flooded through the cracks of the weathered barn walls. Beside Nochka a small rustling drew Nina's eyes from the mare. "Merciful Lord," Nina whispered. She watched in silence as a newborn filly struggled to stand on wobbly legs. Nina stepped back slowly, then turned and ran out of the barn and across the field. She climbed on the woodpile and knocked on Pasha's bedroom window. The curtains moved and Pasha appeared, pushing the window pane open. "What is it, Nina, what's wrong?"

"Come!" she exclaimed.

Pasha met her at the backdoor and ran beside her toward the barn. In the first rays of dawn, the spotted filly stood out like a silhouette. The sun rose behind her, casting its fresh morning light on this little whisper of life.

Pasha froze in place and reached for Nina's hand. "Zorka," he whispered. "Her name is Zorka; since she was born in the early dawn.

"Zorka," Nina echoed. "She came with the first dawn of spring.

The two nodded in agreement.

Pasha's horse Zakhar, the filly's sire, stood at the fence pacing like a nervous parent. "Nice work, Old Boy," Pasha congratulated, "but I think Nochka deserves more of the credit than you do."

The exhausted mare struggled to her feet and nuzzled her newborn with an air of pride and protection.

Pasha glanced at the giant draft-sized hooves on little Zorka. "If she ever grows into those hooves, she will grow up to be a grand workhorse just like her sire. And she'll have twice the gardens to plow since she is owned by both families," Pasha added.

"Only a workhorse?" Nina questioned. "She looks much too noble for a simple plow horse—look at her grand colors, and the way she holds her head. I think she may become a royal mount for the Tsar's Palace Guards."

Pasha laughed and smiled at his young friend. "The Tsar's Palace Guards will be looking for Friesians, not workhorses." Both Pasha's father and brothers were serving as Cossacks in the Imperial

Army under Tsar Nicholas II, as did his Grandfather for Tsar Alexander III. Pasha longed to follow in their footsteps but would have to wait—he was needed too much in the fields. Ever since Nina's father had died, it was Pasha who helped keep her and her Babushka fed and warm, sharing his family's crops and cutting firewood for their stove.

"Well," Nina conceded, "we shall teach Zorka to be loyal and noble none-the-less. Even if it's only to us."

Pasha looked at the filly's unusual spotting and long wobbly legs. "You're right. She shall be Zorka the Loyal and Noble."

Zorka looked over with large innocent eyes at her young masters, then leapt in the air away from her mother's side, trying out her new hindquarters.

"She's a spirited one," Pasha concluded.

"I think she's just showing off for us." Nina laughed. "She will be a strong plow horse one day, but for now, she is our little noble sunrise at dawn."

That afternoon, Nina decided she would surprise Pasha on such a nice spring day. She haltered old Zakhar and tied him to the rail fence, then went inside and packed a picnic lunch. When all was ready, Nina picked up Pasha and they rode double toward the seashore.

Breathing the fresh, salty air, old Zakhar perked right up. He pranced along the shore, then cut across the grassy hill to the meadow that overlooked the Baltic Sea where Nina and Pasha set out the picnic. They let Zakhar graze near-by, who seemed content to stay put, as this was the best grass available for miles.

"Jam?" Nina offered the jar to Pasha. They sat in the meadow on a wool blanket with their warm biscuits. Fresh sweet butter melted and ran like streams down the sides of the biscuits. Nina swirled the homemade jam into pools of melted butter and nibbled at the edges, letting the butter trickle onto her tongue. She closed her eyes and breathed in the sweet spring air. "I love spring," she whispered, reverently.

Pasha glanced over and smiled. "Why?" He enjoyed seeing things through Nina's eyes—her revelations were fresh and intriguing.

"Well," she glanced around, "I see God in everything. I see Him in the tiniest things; the soft, green shoots and the shimmers in the flower petals, and in the way the birds flutter in the sunlight. I hear Him in the whisper of the meadow and the sway of the trees. Sometimes I feel like we're all part of a big sweet chorus." She looked back at Pasha. "You know what I mean?"

Pasha nodded. "I do." He glanced around as though taking in everything Nina had just described. "I'm going to miss all of this one day."

"Miss it?" Nina looked dismayed. "You aren't leaving Rybatskaya?"

"I will have to leave it all one day."

"But, why?"

"To fight for the Tsar of course, along with my father and brothers." He said it so matter of fact that Nina couldn't believe it. It had never dawned on her that such a day would come. Pasha's father and brother had just been home for a long leave. They wouldn't have sent them home if Russia were at war.

"But why, Pasha? There is no war going on."

"But there is much talk of a revolution. My father and brother were just called back. At some point, I will have to fight."

"Why would the common people want a revolution? Why do they dislike the Tsar? Father Nicholai says we're to love our Tsar—that he is a God-fearing man and he loves his Russian people."

"I believe that's true, and you believe that's true, but many people blame him for everything that's going wrong. They feel that because he holds so much wealth and power, he isn't in touch with the people and their sufferings. Some of that may be true, but I believe he truly loves God, and loves and prays for the Russian people."

"What makes people think he doesn't care?"

Pasha sighed. "Well, his reign didn't start off well and some think it was an omen of bad things to come. Have you heard of the tragedy at Khodynka Field?"

"I've heard the name of that field but never really knew what it was about."

"Your Babushka knows. She was at Khodynka Field when it happened. She was lucky to have escaped alive."

"My Babushka?"

"1896 was a horrible time for Russia. The celebration was in honor of the Coronation of Tsar Nicholas ll. Four days after his Coronation they were holding a huge festival to celebrate and The Tsar himself was planning to attend. He sent out announcements that all the people were invited to come to the festival; a huge feast of food, drink, and gifts. They had a special mug made bearing the arms of the city of St. Petersburg and the words 'In memory of the Holy Coronation.' People came from all over Russia—some slept out in the fields waiting for the event to begin. There were thousands of people. But a rumor started that there wouldn't be enough of the mugs to go around and it caused a panic among the people. They began pushing and shoving until it became mayhem. There were lots of holes and ditches in the fields and people were being knocked into them with more people landing on top of them. Pretty soon everyone panicked and began running. Over 1,000 people were trampled to death that day."

Nina stared in shock. "My Babushka was there?"

"She was. She was knocked down and stepped on but your grandfather pulled her up to safety. She has been crippled ever since."

"I never knew. Why has no one ever told me?"

"I'm sure they were waiting until you were old enough to understand."

"But I don't understand. It was all over a stupid mug. I can't understand that, or why they blame the Tsar."

"The problem was, the Tsar was terribly grieved and wanted to cancel the festival following the tragedy, but his advisors fought against it. They said there were too many important people and royalty coming from all over to honor him and they told him to go ahead with the festival. So they did. That angered a lot of people. That was the beginning of people talking against the Tsar and saying it was an omen of things to come—people like Leon Trotsky who hates Imperial Russia. More people have joined his way of thinking since Bloody Sunday.

"I was only five when that happened, but we've learned a lot about it in school since then. They said the Priest Gregory Apollonivich Gapon and hundreds of peasants marched to the Tsar's Winter Palace in St. Petersburg with a petition to try and reason with the Tsar for help because their families were all starving, but he had his Imperial Army shoot them."

"He would never do such a thing!" Nina defended.

"There are two sides to that, too. The revolutionaries disliked the Tsar and Imperial Russia, and made it sound as cold blooded as possible to further their revolutionary causes. But my father told me that the Tsar wasn't even at St. Petersburg at the time and was misinformed of the situation. He didn't realize the peaceful intent behind their protest. He has been trying to reform things until now but a man named Lenin is stirring up all kinds of riots and starting a revolutionary group called the Bolsheviks. My father and brothers say they are going to have a lot of battles on their hands if these groups continue to grow. I have a feeling I may be called to help them fight before too long."

Nina suddenly lost her appetite. "I think I'd like to go home now," she whispered. All she wanted now was to run to the barn and lay in the hay beside Zorka, with her arms wrapped about her neck.

Great Pascha;
Easter
1914

Great Holy Friday

"Today He who hung the earth upon the waters is hung upon the tree.

"The King of angels is decked with a crown of thorns. He who wraps the heavens in a cloud is wrapped in the purple of mockery.

"He who freed Adam in the Jordan is slapped in the face. The Bridegroom of the church is affixed to the cross with nails.

"The Son of the virgin is pierced with a spear.

We worship Thy Passion, O Christ! Show us also Thy glorious resurrection."

Nina could not get her heart around this; God's unfathomable Majesty and extreme humility. It just made her weep. So many things in nature made her feel this way; majesty and power combined with gentleness and tenderness. Majestic Power and Gentle Humility. So many mysteries of God were like this; so beautiful; so sadly, sadly beautiful.

On Resurrection Sunday, known also as Great Pascha, Nina stood near the front of the church between Babushka and Zlata. Zlata had sewn herself a beautiful apron and was wearing it over her skirt. It was a lovely spring day and everyone arrived with baskets filled with brightly died red eggs and sweet bread.

The bountiful baskets were placed on the table before the altar to be blessed by the Priest during the Liturgy. Besides the eggs and bread, there were also meats and cheeses, cakes and cookies for the Pascha feast. All the rich foods they had gone without for the Lenten fast would suddenly reappear on outdoor tables in the meadow to be shared with all.

So important was this day that one would never know there was a shortage of anything to eat in Rybatskaya. Families saved and scrimped, sacrificed and traded in order to bring something special to the table of Great Pascha. Christ is risen! They were there to glorify His resurrection.

As the service came to a close, the door of the church creaked opened. Nina saw all of the color drain from Zlata's face, and turned to the back of the church to see why. A young woman was standing just inside the door holding a toddler. Beneath her faded headscarf and long dark hair, she had a thin, but pretty face. The toddler was small with curly, dark hair, and appeared curious.

"Natalia?" Zlata whispered. Tears streamed down her face as she pushed her way urgently through the assembly of people to reach her long-lost daughter and grandchild. When she finally stood before Natalia, her daughter nearly threw her son into her mother's outstretched arms. "Mama," she sobbed, and wrapped her arms tightly around her mother.

It didn't take long for the congregation to understand who the stranger was, for many of them had known Natalia all throughout her childhood. Aware of the heartache that Zlata had lived with for the past five years, Natalia's return gave great cause for celebration. When Father Nikolai appeared, he recognized her at once. "Praise be to God, our Natalia is home." After he spoke with her briefly, he announced, "It looks as though we will be having a Pascha Baptism after all!"

Everyone ran around preparing the Baptismal for the grandchild, bringing white towels and a small white robe.

Father Nikolai blessed the Baptismal water and anointed the toddler with oil in the name of The Father, The Son, and The Holy Spirit. He recited the prayers of Baptism over him, anointing and sealing him with holy oil. Father Nikolai then immersed him three times under the water and lifted him up, with the name of Petyr.

When little Petyr emerged from the water, everyone sang **"Grant to me a robe of Light as you Clothe yourself in Light, oh Most Merciful Christ Our God."** Nina felt as though the whole church was filled with light. Everyone gathered around the newly illumined child, and warmly welcomed Natalia back home.

Long tables covered in white table linens sat in the middle of a meadow and looked a picture from a royal feast. The tables were all piled high with the decorated baskets. Everyone began to unpack their Paschal delights and spread them out to share with all. Wine bottles were uncorked, glasses were raised, and laughter and singing filled the air. This was a day filled with celebration; of Pascha, of Natalia's homecoming, of Petyr's new life through Baptism, and especially, the Resurrection of Christ! "Christ is risen!" Father Nikolai exclaimed, with a shout.

"Truly He is risen!" the people shouted back.

"I think this is a lovely place to stop, today," Tetushka announced.

Annie sighed. "It's a beautiful story. I hope I can write such stories one day."

Tetushka pulled a slip of paper out of the back of the notebook. It was old, and creased, as though it had been opened and folded many times.

Annie looked intrigued.

"Would you like hear what the author of *Zorka* read many times while he was writing this story?"

Both girls nodded.

"This was written by Archpriest John Iliytch Sergieff, and published 1897. He was also known as the Batiushka of all Russian, Father John of Kronstadt. He reposed in 1908:

"**'On writing:**

"**Do not look upon the printing of a book, but look upon the spirit of the book; otherwise you will depreciate the spirit and exalt the flesh, for the letters are the flesh, and the contents of the book the spirit.'**"

"The spirit of the book,'" Annie repeated. "I like that. I've never thought about it but sometimes when you are reading a story you do sense the spirit of it, don't you?"

Clara nodded. "Especially this book," she added. "I wish we had a writing group at school here. We had one at my old school every Friday."

"Really? Did you belong to it?" Annie asked.

"No, I wanted to, but I joined Cheer Club instead. I really love reading and talking about writing though. I guess I was more worried about being popular."

Tetushka looked thoughtful. "Perhaps you girls could start a club of your own. You know, come once a week and read *Zorka* together. When we've all finished the story, we could have some discussions about the story, the author, and the writing."

The girls looked at each other and agreed full-heartedly.

"Are you sure you don't mind me coming, too?" Annie asked.

"It wouldn't be much of a club with just me," Clara laughed.

"And I certainly don't mind," Tetushka said, "I enjoy the two of you a great deal. How about every Friday then?" Tetushka suggested.

"It's going to be hard to wait a whole week in between, but it will give us something to look forward to," Clara replied.

"What shall we call our little group?" Tetushka asked the girls.

"How about Club Zorka?" Annie offered.

"*Club Zorka*. That's perfect," Clara agreed.

~

Clara told Annie she would walk her back to the

café, just beyond Clara's house. Trudging along in the snow, Annie looked over at Clara, thoughtfully. "It's really strange how much Nina reminds me of myself," she commented. "I mean, losing her parents, then going to live with her aunt. Do you... do you think this all happened for a reason? I mean me and you meeting, and then meeting Tetushka?"

"Tetushka says everything happens for a reason," Clara replied. "I didn't tell you this, because I thought you might think I was weird, but the first day I was here I saw Tetushka in the cemetery praying. After she left, I went over there and when I stood at the gravesite, I had this feeling... like something about that person was... really good. And another thing I noticed: there was a strong fragrance of roses, but there was only one single rose lying by his grave. I wondered how a single red rose could smell like I was standing in a big field of roses."

The two girls looked at one another. "Maybe we'll find out why from reading the story," Annie replied.

~

Saturday morning, Clara's dad announced it was Christmas tree hunting day. A border of trees lined the Bradley's property with plenty of good candidates to choose from. Clara and her brother ran from tree to tree, trying to pick the prize tree. It was the first time Clara ever experienced chopping down her own tree. It reminded her of Nina and Pasha going out to find a tree for Zlata. The day was spent hauling home the biggest tree they could fit into the living room. They decorated all afternoon with their mom while listening to Christmas carols.

It was one of the best weekends Clara had spent with her family since they'd arrived in Bickleton.

The following morning, the phone rang just as Clara was finishing her chores. Annie was inviting her to lunch at Aunt Ruby's café. Clara was excited to see Annie and meet her aunt. She always thought it would be fun to live above a business and just hop down the steps to work. Clara had to admit, it was pretty neat to be able to walk everywhere on her own without having to ask her mom for a ride.

When she reached the café, Annie was waiting out front. "I saved us the best table," she told Clara. "Come on in!"

The girls went inside and grabbed the window booth by the wood stove. Annie handed Clara a menu. "Order anything you like," she exclaimed, "it's on the house!"

"Anything? Really?" Clara's eyes grew big as she scanned the menu.

"That's the best part of living upstairs from a restaurant—you can almost always find something you like whenever you're hungry."

"What's your favorite?" Clara asked.

"The Bickle-burger and fries with a strawberry milkshake. I practically live on that."

"Okay, then, that's what I want too," Clara announced, closing her menu.

Annie's Aunt Ruby swept by their table, noticing the closed menus. "All ready?" she asked. Aunt Ruby's flashy red hair and bright red lipstick and nail polish gave credibility to the name Ruby. "Bet I can guess what y'all are havin'." She pulled her pen and pad from her apron pocket.

"Yep. We'll take two of my usuals, please," Annie replied.

"Two Bickle-burgers, fries, and strawberry shakes it is!" Ruby reached for the closed menus. "And you must be Clara," Ruby confirmed. "It's nice to meet you, Doll. It makes me happy to see my niece do something besides read, read, read!" She snatched up the menus. "Y'all want a pickle with yer Bickle?" She winked, and hustled off toward the kitchen.

"Your aunt is funny," Clara commented.

Annie smiled. "Yeah, my mom always said Aunt Ruby could think and talk twice as fast as my mom when they were kids. She could talk her way out of anything so my mom always got in trouble for whatever her sister did."

Clara was suddenly very aware that Annie had no one but her aunt. "It must be hard...." The words spilled out before she could stop them. Clara was at a loss for what to say next. How do you tell someone that you understand what it's like to lose their family? She couldn't. But she did care. Maybe that was all she needed to say.

Annie looked down. "It is." Then she looked back at Clara. "Thank you," she whispered. "I just haven't been able to tell anyone... until you."

The song "Splish Splash," suddenly bellowed from the old juke box in the corner. "My aunt loves the oldies. She plays them over and over and refuses to update her jukebox. I hear Bobby Darin and Elvis through the heat vents upstairs day in and day out."

"It could be worse," Clara informed her. "My dad listens to Andy Williams and Tony Bennett constantly. If he's not listening to them sing, he's usually singing 'Fly Me to the Moon' himself."

"Two super deluxe strawberry milkshakes for the ladies!" Ruby announced, plopping the tall fountain glasses piled sky high with whipped cream in front of the girls. "Save some of that to go with your burgers." She was gone as fast as she had appeared.

Clara lifted her glass to Annie. "Here's to you, Annie."

Annie clanged her glass with Clara's, and gave her a kind smile. "Here's to new friends. And to *Zorka!*"

"To *Zorka!*" they both cheered.

~

Friday afternoon could not come fast enough for Clara. Tetushka had lent the notebook to Annie to catch up so the girls could read the rest of the story aloud together and discuss the scenes afterwards. Clara didn't realize how hard it was to wait an entire week to continue hearing the story. At lunchtime Friday Clara was looking for Annie but couldn't find her. She was surprised when one of her classmates, Tori, called her over to sit with her and her friends. Tori was one of "the pretty girls," who hung out together and ignored everyone else. Clara reluctantly sat , not sure of their motives. "Hey, is it true you used to be a cheerleader at your old school?" Tori asked.

"Yeah," Clara replied.

"We really want to start a cheer club here. If you want to join us maybe you could teach us some of your cheers."

"Um, sure," Clara replied, feeling flattered they'd asked.

"Hey, why don't you come with us after school to walk around town?" The other two nodded.

Clara was just about to agree when she spotted Annie sitting alone a few tables away and remembered they had plans to read *Zorka*. Maybe she could hang out for a little while before going to Tetushka's. She glanced at Annie. "Do you think my friend, Annie, could come too?"

The group went silent. Tori looked over at Annie. "Her?"

"She's really nice," Clara replied.

"She's not really our type," Tori responded. "Besides, she wouldn't be able to cheer with that gimpy leg of hers, and if we're going to be a team, we need to do things as a team."

Clara had waited a long time to be included by the other girls. She looked at their pretty faces and perfect hair, then back at Annie. "You know," Clara said, "Annie and I have another club we need to meet with today, but thanks." Clara got up, walked to Annie's table, and sat down. "I can't wait to read *Zorka* today!" she exclaimed.

"Me too," Annie replied.

~

Opening the notebook, Tetushka had a twinkle in her eye that caught Clara's attention. "Nina is now fifteen-years-old," she said, "and Pasha is seventeen. They are growing up. Today we will read one of my favorite scenes. Who would like to read aloud?"

"I would," Annie replied; a bit shy, but eager. She began:

Part III

Summer
1914

June

Nina returned *Zorka* to the barn after a long day of tilling soil at Zlata's, for a summer garden. Pasha had left before her, saying he had an appointment. He'd acted vague, which piqued Nina's curiosity to no end. He was usually upfront with her, but lately he just didn't seem himself.

As Nina started for the house, she saw Pasha coming from his cottage. He was wearing a white belted tunic and dark pants that tapered into his black leather boots. He reminded her of a gallant Russian duke, and he had never looked so handsome. Nina watched as he wandered toward the front yard, then saw who his "appointment" was with: the girl whose garden they'd plowed the previous week. The girl with the dyed red hair, who had offered fresh cider to them while they were plowing. Nina had wondered why this girl was so attentive while they worked.

Nina continued her surveillance as Pasha greeted the girl in an openly friendly manner. To Nina's dismay, they started toward the barn and she realized, too late, that she was directly in their path. For the first time, Nina felt awkward around Pasha. He greeted her in an unusually formal way, which irritated her. "Nina, you remember Viktoria?"

Nina was suddenly aware of what a dust-covered urchin she was in comparison to this well-dressed beauty, and nearly tripped on her mud-caked hem while fumbling for Viktoria's delicate outstretched hand.

"A pleasure to see.… " Viktoria graciously began, but faltered when she glanced at the soiled hand Nina offered in return. Viktoria's charming smile wavered, and her hand began to withdraw before Nina was able to grip it.

Nina was horrified. She looked to Pasha for reassurance, but he seemed oblivious to her humiliating encounter. He continued looking gallant, handsome, and oblivious. Nina was furious. She turned and stormed toward her cottage without looking back. She heard Miss Viktoria giggle in response to something Pasha said, and Nina slammed the door behind her. How could he? How could he befriend such a girl? How could he betray their life-long friendship for such a silly girl? She would never speak to him again! Yes, she would… she would speak to him one more time to let him know what a *durak*, idiot, he was to fall for such a shallow-headed nit. Then she never would speak to him again.

The evening hours dragged by. The sun left the summer sky, and a sprinkling of stars replaced the azure blue twilight that Nina loved so much. But tonight she didn't love it. Tonight she hated that Pasha was spending this wondrous mystical moment with someone besides her. Was this something she was going to have to accept as Pasha grew up? Was she going to have to watch her dearest friend fall in love with undeserving girls who knew nothing of his tender heart and pious soul? They would trample on his heart and destroy his fragile soul. How could she go on knowing this was the fate of a man in the hands of a worldly girl? Why did her dear Pasha have to be so naive? Nina's thoughts raged and drowned out every attempt her soul made to quiet her thoughts. Instead, Nina watched from beneath the apple tree in the orchard for the first stirring of dust down the long still road that Pasha would tread home.

Finally, a dark silhouette came down the lane toward her. Nina did not want to appear too anxious or ridiculous, both of which she had spent the entire day doing. As Pasha approached the orchard, she quickly made an attempt to appear busy.

"Picking apples in the moonlight? Pasha teased.

Nina tried to look surprised at his arrival, and turned with her apron full of apples, hoping to validate her excuse. "I thought it was a nice evening to make apple butter."

"Did you?" he glanced at the apples gathered in her apron with a raised brow.

He didn't believe her. She knew it, but she didn't

care. "And how was your evening with Miss Viktoria?" It took great effort to say her name sweetly, a little too sweet, she feared.

Pasha smiled. "The moonlight was brilliant on the sea tonight."

"You walked by the sea?" How dare he? That was her sea, not Viktoria's.

"We walked along the shore barefoot and collected shells, then sat beneath the stars on that log you and I carved our names in." He looked away wistfully.

Nina's cheeks burned. Our log? He sat on our log with her and did what? Just because Nina was only fifteen didn't mean that she didn't understand things between a boy and girl. But for Pasha to throw himself at a girl like that... The image stoked her fury.

Pasha touched her arm lightly, "Oh, little Ninka, one day you will grow up and fall in love and then you will understand these matters of romance."

That did it. She jerked her arm away. "I understand plenty at my age, but if you are too blind to see through a weak and worldly girl then you deserve her!" Nina dropped her apron hem, and turned to go. The apples rolled in all directions.

Pasha pulled Nina around to face him. His teasing eyes turned sympathetic and gentle. "I'm sorry, Nina. I was just having a little fun. Don't worry—I saw what kind of girl Viktoria was the moment she pulled her hand away from greeting you. Any girl who looks down on my Ninochka for plowing a field all day or who cannot laugh when she is thrown into the sea, as you do, is not worthy of my affections."

"You tossed her into the sea?" Nina fought back a smile.

"It was only meant as a playful little push, but she tripped. She didn't take it the way you do." He smiled tenderly. "I promise, Ninochka, I won't fall in love with any girl without your approval." He looked away, and shook his head. "She was a spoiled little thing!" He turned to go, but looked back with a handsome grin. "It's late; you'd better get to bed. Thanks for waiting up for me."

Tetushka looked up and smiled. Annie blushed and Clara giggled.

"Is there anything you see in Nina that you notice in other girls these days?"

"Jealousy!" Clara exclaimed. "Girls are always jealous of other girls when it comes to boys."

Annie thought a little longer. "Well, there is something I noticed about Nina that I do myself sometimes."

"What is that?" Tetushka asked.

"She kind of lets her imagination run away sometimes."

"Ah, you saw that?" Tetushka looked pleased.

"The more time you have to think about something, the worse it seems to get."

"Yes, our thoughts are powerful, for good or bad. We can spend a lot of time worrying about things that are neither true nor ever really happen."

Clara nodded, thoughtfully.

Tetushka went to the kitchen and returned with

tea and scones. She set the tray before the girls, who were growing accustomed to helping themselves to both. "We will have some history to discuss next time we meet," Tetushka told them. "The Russian-German war is coming soon. You two might be interested in learning about that."

"Yes," Clara replied, "but not too much history. I like the romance parts the best." Both girls giggled.

Tetushka laughed. "I'll tell you what? There is one more small romantic scene before we get into the war history. Pasha was reaching an age that young Russian ladies began to notice boys. Russian girls married quite young and they needed to find a good provider. The more handsome the boy, the more attention he began to receive. And Pasha.... well, Pasha was the most handsome boy in town." The two girls looked at each other and blushed.

This did not go unnoticed by Tetushka. "Let's get the romance out of the way today and save the history for next week."

"Yes!" Both girls agreed, laughing.

"I can read this time," Clara announced.

"All is fair in love and war," Annie replied, and handed the notebook to Clara.

July 1914

As the Sunday picnic spread into the surrounding meadow, Nina noticed a new face in the crowd. She hadn't recognized her until she took off her head scarf, and her long, wavy, dark hair fell to her waist. Until now, Nina's hair had been the longest in the church—which she secretly took pride in. But Nina's hair was straight. This girl also had big brown eyes. Apparently, Nina wasn't the only one who noticed. Three or four of the older boys were working their way toward her, Pasha among them.

Nina was not going to fall into jealousy this time, the way she had with Viktoria. Pasha at least saw through Viktoria. If there was something about this new girl that was not of good character, she had every confidence that Pasha would notice. Hopefully. But, what if she did have virtues worthy of someone like Pasha; what then? If nothing else, she hoped Pasha noticed the girl had ugly shoes.

She realized she was over-thinking things, and went to get a plate of food. She began to feel stupid for assuming so much, and scolded herself for letting her imagination run away. Again. She told herself to stop acting immature.

"Nina?"

She turned abruptly and found herself face-to-face with Pasha and the new girl. "Oh, hello."

"My mother is busy talking with Father Nikolai. Would you let her know I'm walking Anastasia home and I won't be home until later?"

"How much later?" Nina asked. "...so I can tell your mother, I mean."

"Quite a bit later," Pasha replied. "I'll try to be home by supper."

Anastasia responded with a beautiful smile.

Nina responded with a headache. "Fine. I'll tell her." She was no longer hungry. She set her plate down, turned away, and trudged toward home. Why did these girls have to keep throwing themselves at Pasha? "Viktoria, Anastasia....who's next?" she muttered under her breath. Nina secretly hoped this girl would turn out to be as silly as the last one so she and Pasha could get back to being best friends. Now instead of walking home with Pasha along the shore, she'd have nothing to do all day. Zlata would be busy with her daughter and grandson, so visiting them was out. Babushka's ankles would be sore after her morning at church. She would just want to rest for the afternoon.

Nina decided to spend the day at the barn with the horses. She found a sunny spot on top of some hay bales, and fell asleep.

~

Nina heard footsteps beside her and realized she'd slept the afternoon away.

"Hey, sleepyhead." Pashas' voice awoke her.

"Hey," she mumbled back, eyes blinking back the bright sunlight.

Pasha sat beside her on the warm hay bale, where she remained curled in a ball. He smiled down at her.

"How was your day with Anastasia?" Nina asked, casually.

Pasha looked thoughtful. "It was... pleasant," he replied.

This got her attention. She raised herself on her elbows and rested her head in her hands. "Pleasant?" Nina hated to sound so curious but there was no way around it.

"Pleasant," he repeated.

She wanted it translated into how long it would be before it was just she and Pasha. Without all of these darn girls interrupting their friendship.

"Are you going to spend more time with her?" Nina blurted. "I mean, will I have to plow gardens alone?"

Pasha looked intently at Nina. "You know, Nina, it might not be a bad idea for you to learn to plow without me—there may come a time when I won't be here to help you, and you will need to know how."

Nina turned toward Pasha. Desperate. "Not be here—what do you mean, not be here? You aren't going to marry her, are you?"

Pasha laughed. "Of course, I'm not going to marry

her! I meant there are things changing with the country; people are talking of war and revolution, and no one knows what is going to happen next. I want you to be able to survive if anything should happen to me."

Nina froze at the thought of something happening to Pasha that might leave her alone. "You can't leave me," she began. "You can't leave me and Babushka, and your own mother alone—what will we do without you?" She was on the brink of tears.

Pasha placed his hand on her shoulder. "I'm sorry I worried you. I'm not going anywhere for now. It will be okay. Whatever happens, God will take care of us. Today, we have no war. Please don't worry."

Nina realized Pasha was right. Today there was no war. She still had Pasha beside her, and that was enough for now.

Pasha gave her a reassuring smile. "I'm going to wash up. I'll see you at supper."

~

The trees in the orchard were loaded with fragrant fruit. As evening fell, Babushka and Liliya set a table by the pond to have supper. It was cool and shady beneath the trees with a gentle breeze. Nina had just come from picking the early summer lettuce. She changed into a yellow and white summer dress she'd made with Zlata's help, and was proud of the way it turned out.

Nina sat beneath the tree, winding a bright yellow ribbon through her dark, shiny mane, then wove it all into a long, thick braid. Catching her reflection in the pond, she had to admit she felt pretty.

As she filled glasses from a water pitcher, Pasha appeared in the orchard, walking toward her. He was wearing a clean white tunic contrasting his dark hair, combed back from his tanned face. The instant his soft gaze caught Nina's, her heart fluttered. For the first time, she had an acute awareness that Pasha was not her brother, or even just her friend. He was someone far more endearing.

At the same time, Pasha slowed his pace, coming to a near stand-still without taking his gaze from Nina. The only thing that snapped Nina back was the overflowing glass of water in her hand. Pasha glanced at the spilled water, and smiled.

"Pasha, would you ask the blessing?" his mother said, helping Babushka to her seat.

"Uh, sure." He glanced away, but he and Nina knew something had passed between them.

Pasha crossed himself, and led the Our Father. From that point on, he and Nina spent the rest of the meal trying to act as though everything was just as it had always been. A comforting thought crossed her mind. She was no longer jealous of Anastasia. Something inside knew that what passed between herself and Pasha was theirs alone. Her thoughts drifted to a bigger fear. War. The one thing that could still separate them. Would their bond transcend distance and time?

When the meal ended, Nina started clearing dishes. Pasha lingered patiently at the table after his mother and Babushka had gone inside. When Nina went to take his plate, he stood and gently clasped her hand causing her to look at him. "What's wrong, Nina?"

She looked away, "Nothing."

Pasha looked amused. He continued to hold her hand, not taking his eyes from hers. "I don't believe you. You're worried about something, aren't you?"

He was unbearably close and Nina felt herself blush, something she had never done in front of him. "Why should I be worried?" she replied.

"That's what I'd like to know." His gaze lingered as he gently released her hand.

Nina didn't move. She just stared, barely breathing.

"Ninochka," he whispered.

Nina saw all she needed to know in his eyes. His heart belonged to her. Time or distance could not touch what she felt inside.

~

The lace curtains in Nina's bedroom danced in the warm, summer breeze. It carried the scent of roses that grew below her window. She could hear the soft rustle through the trees and a soothing peace filled her soul. It was a strange new feeling; sweet, and gentle. She drifted into a lovely dream of dancing through a meadow. But in her dream, she was not dancing alone.

August 1, 1914

Nina awoke with the soft light of dawn and set out toward the barn. She noticed movement in Pasha's home. Her heart skipped a beat at the thought of his name. She watered and fed the horses, then returned and poured herself a cup of tea. As she sat down at the table, there was a light knock at the door, followed by a push on the door. Pasha walked in.

Nina knew the instant she saw his face something was wrong. "Pasha, what is it?"

Pasha crossed the room and stood in front of Nina who had risen. "Germany has just declared war on Russia."

"War? We are at war with Germany?" Nina felt the blood rush from her face and she became light-headed.

Pasha reached for her hand and clasped it tightly. "Ninochka, I must go. I must fight for Russia."

"Go? Leave us?" Nina's legs gave way and she grabbed onto both of Pasha's arms to steady herself.

Pasha's strong grip held her tight. "I need to take Zorka. She is the only horse strong enough to go."

"Zorka? My Zorka?" Nina's face fell even further. "But who will care for us, Pasha? How will we survive?"

Pasha looked deep into Nina's eyes, and continued to hold her near. "You are a strong, brave woman, Ninochka. You and my mother and Babushka will work together. The older men in the town are staying—ask for their help when you need it. And Father Nikolai—he will help you the most—go to him, often." A pained look crossed his face as he moved away. "I must go—I need to gather my things and prepare Zorka for our journey."

"I will get Zorka ready," Nina left, and ran toward the barn.

An hour later Pasha returned with his duffle bag, heavy boots, and winter jacket—which seemed out of place for August, but everyone knew what was ahead if the war continued into the winter months. Soldiers who were not prepared would freeze to death.

Zorka was tied to the railing and Nina stood at her side stroking her soft neck for the last time. "Be brave my little Zorka," she whispered. "Bring my Pasha back to me."

Zorka nuzzled Nina's head, which only brought Nina to the brink of tears. She watched Pasha from the corner of her eye as he embraced his mother, who ran back into the house, sobbing. Pasha turned and strode toward Nina. She could not bear to look at him holding his duffle bag. She refused to remember him that way.

Pasha sensed her reluctance, set down his bag, and went to her. An endless stream of tears began to fall, but she fought to keep her gaze on him, knowing it might be the last glance ever to pass between them. She felt his hand on her cheek as he gently wiped away her tears. "Don't cry, Ninochka, I will come back."

She nodded.

Pasha held her face in both his hands. He looked deep into her eyes, "Wait for me." He tore himself away and mounted Zorka.

"Pasha!" She ran to Zorka's side and handed something to him. "Remember me," she said. Pasha slipped the wood rabbit into his coat pocket, then turned, and galloped down the long dusty road without looking back. Nina watched until the last cloud of dust settled on the horizon.

~

The following Friday, Clara and Annie arrived, eager to learn some Russian war history. Tetushka appeared deep in thought as she stared at the pages ahead of them. "Now," she said softly, "I will tell you, the war was very difficult for both those left to survive without the men, and the men fighting away from home. Winters on the front were bitterly cold and war is cruel. Russia's Imperial Army was loyal to the Tsar, and even though he did not want war, Germany was aggressive. Thousands of lives were lost on both sides. Initially, Russia had some small victories, but the German army had superior weapons and supplies. The war took a big toll on Russia; the army's food supplies and ammunition ran short, and many soldiers were left on the battlefield without enough of either."

Winter at War
1914-1915

Without the men in Rybatskaya, the town became like a ghost town. The women had to pull together to get the harvest in before the first cold snap or all would have been lost in the way of their winter food storage. Potatoes had to be dug, fruit hand-picked and canned, fields cut and bailed to supply the livestock with hay for the winter ahead. Many of the horses had gone off with the soldiers, leaving only Nochka and Old Zakhar to help with the work.

Nina, Babushka, and Pasha's mother joined forces and worked with Father Nikolai to try and meet their own needs, as well as help the widows and elderly in the church. It wasn't unusual to see women harnessed to pull a plow across a garden or field in place of the horses. Women chopped wood, repaired homes, carried heavy sacks of grain, and hauled loads of coal and wood to heat their homes.

By the end of the harvest, Nina had worked herself to the bone. Rather than try and heat three separate homes, by mid-winter Nina, Babushka, Liliya, Zlata, her daughter and grandchild would often huddle together in one cottage around the fireplace and conserve resources as long as possible. They would cook together, eat together, and sleep together, piling all of their blankets and furs beside the fire to keep from freezing. They were good company during such times.

Many of the women went to church every day to pray for their men. Nina was among them. Father Nicholai was her only voice of hope. There were many funerals during those dark days, and many broken hearts. "Keep praying," Father Nicholai encouraged, "your prayers are more powerful than war. Love conquers hate."

The people at home were desperate for word from the front, but news only came by way of nearby villagers when someone was wounded and sent home from battle.

How Nina longed for a word or letter from Pasha. She would give anything for one of Pasha's fairytales. No matter how bad life could get, memories of his stories always cheered her. But the memories began to fade along with her dreams.

As the long winter turned to spring, and spring turned to summer, Nina tried to stay hopeful, but when the trees began to drop their leaves and the summer flowers began to die, so did her hopes of ever hearing from Pasha.

Fall 1915

At daybreak, Nina heated water outside for the day's chores. It was wash day and it would take time for the water to get hot. She methodically planned her day, keeping an eye on the bubbles accumulating at the bottom of the wash tub. In the first ray of sunlight, she noticed a plume of dust in the distance. Her thoughts and plans came to a standstill. She watched as it moved slowly up the long dirt road toward her farm. She began to make out the form of a man, and as he came closer, his slow gait. She waited. "Pasha?" she whispered. Nina abandoned her wash tub, and ran up the lane. As she got closer, she could see the uniform of a Cossack. "Pasha!" she cried, and ran breathlessly toward him. Just before she reached him, he fell to the ground.

Nina threw herself beside his wounded body. When she saw his face, disappointment took hold. It was not her Pasha. It was a soldier, but not her soldier.

The soldier moaned, snapping Nina from despair to the realization that this wounded man needed help, regardless of who he was. "I'll be right back." She ran toward Pasha's home, knowing Pasha's mother would think this stranger was her son. Nina had to warn her before she saw him. Nina slid inside and called for Liliya. When she appeared, Nina explained quickly, "It's a wounded soldier—he needs our help."

The two women returned to the wounded man. They wrapped each of his arms around their shoulders, then dragged him into Pasha's house where they laid him on the couch near the stove. He was not conscious, but he was alive. Nina pulled off his boots while Liliya got hot water from the stove and some rags. He was crusted in dried blood and dirt, and they couldn't know how bad it was until they cleaned him up.

When Nina went to remove his jacket, she checked his pockets for hints of who he might be. She reached in and felt something smooth and familiar: the wood rabbit she gave to Pasha when he left for the war. What was this man doing with Pasha's rabbit? It made no sense. They needed to get him well enough to tell them who he was and what he knew of Pasha.

When all of the wounds had been cleaned and wrapped, Nina tried to hold his head up, hoping to wake him and get some warm broth down him. As she held his head steady and began to pour, his mouth closed around the lip of the mug and he made the effort to drink. He coughed and sputtered, but opened his eyes. They came to focus on Nina's face and he strained and squinted in the bright morning light. "Nina?" he whispered.

"How do you know me?"

"Pasha...." He said weakly, "Pasha told me to come."

"P-Pasha sent you to me? Where is Pasha?"

The soldier's eyes closed and he winced in pain. "We got hit—Pasha and me. Grenades. Pasha is bad. He.... couldn't get up. He told me to come to you .... said you would help me and that I was to help your family and his." He winced again, "I'm Mikhail." He went silent.

Nina covered Mikhail with a blanket and sat beside him. She realized after he was washed and cleaned that he resembled Pasha in neither looks nor coloring. His hair and skin were fairer, and she decided he was from a different part of Russia. As she stared at him sleeping, she picked up the small wood rabbit and held it tight. Pasha was the last one to have touched it and he'd sent it back to her. She didn't want the rabbit and she didn't want the soldier. She only wanted Pasha, and only the Lord knew where he was now... or if he still lived.

~

It was a good diversion from war and worry for the three women to become pre-occupied with saving this soldier. Their days were spent cooking for him and dressing his wounds. They felt Mikhail was their connection to Pasha, and they doted over him with great care. In time, Mikhail grew stronger and helped the women who had nursed him back to health. To have a man around to do the heavy lifting and difficult chores they had struggled to do was a relief. The four of them worked well as a team and life worked into somewhat of a manageable routine, rather than a desperate mode of survival.

As Nina and Mikhail often worked side by side, they developed a comfortable friendship. Mikhail was a good and kind man. Nina began to understand why Pasha had sent him. She still would rather that Mikhail were Pasha, and prayed constantly for his return.

Mikhail shared some details of the war, sparing some of his more painful memories. He told of Russia's few victories in the beginning, and sadly, their many losses. "We out-numbered them in the beginning, but the Germans were a brutal force to be up against. As we began to run short of ammunition and supplies, they brought in weapons we'd never seen before. Russia couldn't keep up with their production. Our shortages got so bad, some men were sent to the front without a gun and told to find one off the fallen soldiers."

There were times Mikhail could not speak at all and his mind seemed to be in another place. One such night over dinner, Nina asked, "What do you think about when you seem to drift away in your mind?"

Mikhail drew his attention back to Nina and sighed. "Comrades; friends. The ones I lost."

Nina shivered. She had been too afraid to ask before, but she had to ask now. "Do you think Pasha had any chance?"

Mikhail looked down. "...I don't think so," he whispered. His eyes averted hers. "The Germans were throwing hand-grenades into our trenches.

Pasha pushed me away. He saved me. But he took the worst of the blow himself. I... I tried to stay to help him, but was commanded to go. He said your name. I knelt to listen. 'Help Nina. Help my mother.' He reached in his pocket and handed me something to give you... the rabbit. I grabbed it and ran....then heard another blast behind me. I didn't, couldn't look back." Mikhail choked up. "I just kept running."

Nina never asked again.

~

As winter melted into spring, Nina and Mikhail began to plow for the first spring planting. The ground was rich and fertile beneath the thawing snow. Not everyone was fortunate to have survived the winter. People and livestock died from hunger all over Russia. The women were grateful that Mikhail had come, as were many of the other women he had helped in their town.

As the days grew warmer, Nina realized something she didn't want to face. She knew Mikhail had a family of his own in Moscow. He had stayed to see these women through the winter in gratitude for their nursing him back to health, as well as for the soldier who had saved his life. Mikhail had mentioned when he first came that he would travel home once the weather warmed. Something inside Nina did not want him to leave. She wasn't sure if it was because Mikhail was her sole connection to Pasha, or if it was his company she would miss. She began to think it was both.

One afternoon after the two finished planting potatoes, they decided to take a walk along the shore. "Do you miss your family?" Nina asked.

Mikhail grew thoughtful. "Sometimes," he replied. He looked at Nina with kind eyes. "I will miss being here when I go," he added.

"What is your family like?"

Some of the warmth drained from his eyes. "I was never close to my parents. I was basically raised by my Babushka, but she is gone now." He looked sad. "My parents were very busy in political things. They traveled a lot, and I saw little of them growing up. I miss my brothers and sister, but they have families of their own."

"What will you be going back to?"

Mikhail looked toward the horizon. "I won't be going home to much," he replied. "I will be taking on some of my father's affairs, as he owns a large estate he has passed to me to oversee. But as far as family goes, not much."

Nina felt sorry for Mikhail having no one whom he felt close to. "Do you need to return soon to take over the affairs?"

"I will eventually need to, but since no one really knows where I am or when this war will end, I'm not in a rush. You could say, no one is expecting me."

Nina felt strangely relieved. She did not like the feeling of abandonment on any level; be it her parents, her baby sister, Pasha, or now, Mikhail. Why did people always have to leave her? "Will you stay a little longer?"

Mikhail looked at Nina and dared to look into her eyes when he asked, "Do you want me to stay?"

"Yes," she said quietly, and looked toward the sea.

"Then I will."

The two walked along in silence for a long time, neither sensing the need to talk, or turn back. They arrived home at dusk to a worried grandmother. "Where have you been?" Babushka asked.

"Just walking," Nina replied, busying herself. Mikhail made a hasty exit to carry in some firewood.

"Just walking?" Babushka repeated to herself, and continued to stir a large pot of borsht.

Tetushka looked at Clara and Annie. "What do you think of the friendship between Mikhail and Nina?" She asked.

Clara didn't appear as bothered as Annie. "I think it seems natural they would grow close. They spend so much time together trying to survive, and he is the only one around who's Nina's age."

"How about you Annie, what do you think?"

"I don't know…. It bothers me. I mean, it's okay if they want to be friends, but it bothers me that Nina might be falling for Mikhail. I guess I believe more in true love and loyalty. Even if Pasha did die, she should still wait and make sure before she lets herself fall for Mikhail."

Tetushka nodded. "Does it seem in Nina's character to look to someone else for strength or companionship?"

"Maybe for strength or companionship, but not for a relationship when she still loves Pasha," Annie replied.

Clara jumped in, "Not under normal circumstances, but I think war can change people. I mean if I were alone and scared and a nice, handsome soldier was always helping me and my family, you can't really say what you would do unless it happened to you."

"Just reading what war was like," Annie added, "makes me see how lucky we are that we've never had to live through things like that. I have been feeling sorry for myself that I lost my family, but I still have a nice aunt and a warm home with food, and you two for friends. Nina lost her family, and her best friend, and people are freezing, and starving all over Russia".

"You're right, Annie," Tetushka replied. "We need to remember to be thankful for what we have, rather than focus on what we don't have. We are fortunate to be living in freedom and without constant fear. I came to America to escape the constant fear and evil that the Bolsheviks cast on Russia. They killed our people, our Priests and Bishops, and tried to destroy our churches." Tetushka suddenly looked very tired, and suggested they all meet again the following week to finish the story.

"It's hard to wait," Clara said, "on the other hand, I don't want the story to end."

"Me neither," Annie agreed. "I'm going to miss this so much."

"Perhaps we can find another book to read after this," Tetushka suggested.

"Yeah, or maybe we can write a sequel to Zorka!" Clara laughed.

"Maybe." Tetushka smiled.

~

Clara and Annie couldn't stand the wait, and

dropped by Tetushka's two days later. "Can we finish the story today?" they pleaded.

Spring 1916

Nina had finished her afternoon gardening. She knew Babushka would need fresh milk for her baking. Mikhail was at the end of the lane, on his way to Zlata's to chop firewood for her.

Nina started toward the barn to do the milking. Glancing over the steppe, her eye caught movement in the distance. Squinting toward the sunlight, she made out the form of a horse. It advanced at an unsteady pace. With the sunlight behind it, Nina caught a glimpse of its unusual contrasting coat of brown and white, with a jet black mane and tail. "Zorka?" she breathed, softer than a whisper. She didn't dare say it louder for fear it might vanish.

The horse barely lifted its head, dragging its hooves up the dusty road with effort. Nina froze in her steps and watched as the sun illuminated the lighter shades of its coat against the dark black. "Zorka!" She dropped her milking can and flew toward, a sight that she begged God, was real.

Coming closer, Nina realized there was no rider, only saddle bags, and her heart sank. Moving closer still, she realized that what she saw as saddle bags was really the form of a soldier lying face down across the saddle. "Pasha!" she cried. Zorka's head rose at the sound of Nina's voice and whinnied weakly in response. Her gait picked up, straining hard to reach Nina.

Nina ran toward her beloved horse and soldier, tears streaking her face. Reaching Zorka, she flew to her side. The soldier lay motionless across the saddle, arms hanging limp at Zorka's bony side. Nina took the soldier's head in her hands and gently turned his face toward her. "Pasha."

His eyes remained closed.

Nina wasn't the only one who had watched with undying hope as the horse ambled down the dusty road. As soon as Liliya caught sight of the wounded soldier from her kitchen window, she too, ran to his side, crying hysterically.

Nina led Zorka toward the house where the two women found the strength to carry Pasha into his home and lay him on the bed in the back room. He made a faint moan as they straightened his wounded body on the bed. While Liliya went to gather hot water and rags, Nina gently touched Pasha's face, just to make sure he was real. Even with his hair caked in mud, and face streaked with blood, he was beautiful to her. She buried her face in his neck and sobbed his name over and over, until she heard a soft whisper, "Ninochka."

Mikhail had returned from Zlata's and heard the news from Babushka. Out of respect for Nina and Pasha's mother he kept his distance while they reunited. He tended Zorka's wounds in the barn, wrapping her legs with warm compresses.

After supplying hot water and rags for Nina, Liliya went to the kitchen to prepare some warm broth for her son, leaving Nina alone to tend to the dressings. Pasha had not spoken or stirred since he'd said her name, but, thankfully, still breathed. Nina looked upon his worn, handsome face, taking in every detail she had missed so much. Even with all the cuts and scrapes, no one had ever looked so beautiful.

The majority of the serious wounds appeared to be in his lower extremities. Nina washed Pasha's lacerations and scrubbed away old, dried blood with the warm, soapy water, then wrapped them with clean bandages made from strips of old bed sheets. She prayed over him continually as she worked, "Lord Jesus, have mercy on my Pasha." Completing the bandaging, she laid her head on his chest and remained there until she fell asleep.

In the midst of a strange dream, Nina felt a hand clasping hers. It jolted her awake. Nina lifted her head and found herself gazing into the depths of the ice blue eyes she'd so longed for. "Pasha," she whispered.

He reached his bandaged hand to her face and placed it gently on her cheek. "Are you real this time?"

Nina's eyes filled with tears. She pressed his

hand to her lips and kissed his palm. "I'm real."

"My Ninochka," he whispered, then closed his eyes, and fell silent again.

When Pasha awoke hours later, it was early morning. Nina lay by his side, still holding his hand. The gentle light of dawn filtered through the curtains and landed softly on Nina's sweet face as she slept. He smiled that she was still beside him and hadn't vanished like a dream as she had so many times before. His smile suddenly turned to a grimace, and the jolt from his pain caused Nina to stir.

"What's wrong, Pasha?"

"My leg. I think there may be shrapnel in there."

"We've sent for the doctor, but aren't sure when he will get here."

He looked at Nina. "Could you give me a kiss just in case he doesn't get here in time?"

Nina looked worried. "What do you mean, 'in case he doesn't get here I time'?" Is it really that bad?"

The creases near Pasha's eyes crinkled, "I thought I might get a kiss if I put it that way."

Nina smiled, then blushed. She was considering how to go about it without hurting Pasha. Before she had time to figure it out, Pasha took her face between his two bandaged hands and tenderly kissed her instead.

Nina felt warm and dizzy at the same time. She gently laid her head on Pasha's chest, and closed her eyes. "Please tell me a story," she whispered. "I've so missed your stories, Pasha."

Pasha rested his bandaged arm gently upon

Nina's back, and in a soft, quiet, familiar voice, began: "There once lived a beautiful young Duchess with hair as dark as night, skin as fair as the pale moon, and eyes the color of emeralds."

"What color is her dress?" Nina whispered.

"What's your favorite color?"

"Green. Like a meadow in spring."

"That's good, because that's exactly what she was wearing."

Nina smiled.

"One day, a young soldier rode his noble war horse home from battle, and passed through a small village by the sea. He saw this fair maiden dancing alone with closed eyes, in a big green meadow. He watched her for a long time, until she sensed a pair of eyes upon her. Startled, she found herself staring into the eyes of a brave, young warrior returning from war."

"Was he handsome?"

"Extremely."

"Were his eyes blue?" Nina whispered.

"Intensely."

Nina smiled.

"Well, the soldier bowed to the maiden and said to her, "Fair Maiden, did you know that while I lay injured on a battlefield for many days, I dreamt of nothing but you? When I was hungry, the remembrance of you filled my very heart and soul. And when I was cold and felt I'd freeze in that cold, lonely field, the thought of your smile warmed me. And when I felt too weak to move and try to save myself, your prayers found me and I awoke to your noble and loyal horse, who stayed beside me until I found the strength to pull myself across her saddle. Then by God's grace, she found her way home."

Nina could not speak or move. She lay completely still, listening to his beating heart, while her tears fell upon the chest of her very brave, very handsome soldier.

Nina was afraid to open her eyes. She would rather go on dreaming than to find out this moment wasn't real.

There was a gentle knock on the door. Nina reluctantly sat up. "The doctor must be here," she said. "Come in."

Pasha looked over as the door opened. "Mikhail....?"

~

The two men were left to reunite. Nina waited, nervously, not knowing exactly what she was nervous about. She only knew an awkward tension began to permeate the house. Pasha was in fact a war hero to Mikhail, but there were now two men in the house and one Nina, and for some reason, things did not feel right.

During his recovery over the next few weeks, Pasha spent a good deal of time visiting with Father Nikolai. Father was a great comfort to him after all he had seen in war, as he had fought in war as a young man himself. It was hard for Pasha to talk about it with anyone else. As Pasha's health progressed and he began to converse more, Nina spent a lot of time at the side of his bed, cleaning, feeding, and talking with him. Mikhail immersed himself in the outside chores and more or less kept some distance. It seemed apparent once Pasha was back on his feet, Mikhail would have his own home and affairs to tend to.

As Pasha began to move about, it was clear his right leg was far from healed, and he continued to walk with a severe limp that required the aid of a crutch. The few visits from the village doctor confirmed extensive damage to his upper thigh that would likely never heal completely. A fair amount of shrapnel had been removed, leaving a good deal of muscle and bone permanently maimed.

As time passed, Mikhail did not mention leaving, yet he and Pasha barely spoke to one another. Nina was aware that things seemed strained between the two, but she wasn't entirely sure why until the night they entered the barn while she was stooped down milking Krem in her stall.

"I realize you saved my life, Pasha, and I'm grateful. I came here because you told me to look after Nina and your mother, and I did. I did not expect to fall in love with Nina, but I have."

"You don't even know her," Pasha replied.

"I know you love her too, Pasha, but she loves me now. She even told me to stay."

There was a long, silent pause.

Mikhail continued, "If you truly love her, you would see that I have more to offer her than you. My family has land, and wealth. She would have the best of everything and never be in want again. All you can offer her is... is... this...." he said, with disdain, as though their home town held nothing of worth. "If you really love her, would you not want the best for her?"

"Are you saying you're the best for her? You and

your land? You, who know nothing about her heart or soul? Where were you when her parents and sister died and she had no one to look after her and her Babushka? Or when she ran through these meadows and saw God in everything here? Were you here when she held out her hand and small birds perched in her palm and ate crumbs without fear? I was. I was here. I saw things that no other eyes but Nina's and God's have seen. You say you love her, and yet you would take her from the very place she loves, the only place she now considers home?"

"She will die if she stays here with you. How will you feed her and care for her? You're a cripple. Will you really be that selfish?"

Pasha looked down at his leg, then slowly raised his gaze, where it froze on Mikhail's. "I may be crippled, and I may have little wealth to offer, but I know the heart of the one you say you love, and if you think your land and money will make Nina happy, you're a bigger fool than I. This war is not between you and me. Nina has a mind and a heart of her own. She will be the one who decides who and what she wants, and you and I will have no say in it."

"Fine," Mikhail replied, in an icy tone. "May the best fool win."

Nina listened as a pair of heavy boots marched away and the barn fell silent. She peered through the slats of wood in the stall. Pasha sat on a hay bale, his crutch lying at his foot. His eyes were cast down, staring at his crippled leg. Then, with great effort, he grabbed his crutch, rose to a stand, and limped out of the barn, turning toward the church.

Nina quietly stepped out of the stall and went quickly in search of Mikhail.

When Pasha returned, he saw Nina and Mikhail heading down the lane with duffle bags in hand.

"Pasha," his mother said, as he entered the house, "Mikhail has gone home." Pasha turned and headed for the barn.

When Pasha entered the barn, he went to Zorka and wrapped his arms around her neck and mane. He reached in his pocket and brought out a carrot he'd pulled for her, then sat on the bale of hay to rest his leg. Pasha heard the sound of footsteps coming toward him. He raised his head, his gaze set on Nina. "You're still here," he said.

"Where else would I be?"

"I thought...."

"That I left with Mikhail?" Nina looked hurt. "I walked him to the end of the lane to say good bye."

"He said you love him and told him to stay."

Nina's eyes teared up, but she said nothing.

"Is it true?"

"I told him to stay because I was lonely and he was my friend. I never loved him." Nina looked into Pasha's sad, deep eyes. "Pasha..." she stepped toward him and kneeled at his side. "...don't you know I have always loved only you?"

"But I have nothing to offer you. Look at me. I'm crippled."

"We are all crippled, Pasha... some inwardly, some outwardly. What does that have to do with loving someone?"

"How can I ask you to marry me now? I can't even walk."

Nina looked at Pasha. "Haven't you ever heard the story of Stumblelinka?"

Pasha looked at Nina with a sweet, sad smile. "I wish my silly little fairytales could help me now. I'm not even able to dance with my Duchess."

Nina glanced over at Zorka watching from her stall. "Now that Zorka is too lame to plow is she less of a horse to you?"

Pasha was taken aback by Nina's question. "Of course not. She gave everything she had out of loyalty. How could she ever mean less to me now? She means a great deal more to me now."

Nina looked at Pasha and smiled. "Just because you can't walk, and you can't dance, doesn't mean you can't hold me and love me forever."

Pasha pulled Nina into his arms. "Forever is a long time…. I guess we'd better get started."

Clara and Annie looked at each other and sighed. Then they looked at Tetushka. "Come, I want to show you something," she said. "Grab your coats."

The girls followed Tetushka to the graveyard. Standing before Pavel's wood cross she asked, "So, now that you have read Pavel's story what have you discovered about him?"

"Pavel must have been a good soul," Clara replied.

"What makes you think that?" Tetushka asked.

"When I first came to his grave, I felt like I was surrounded by goodness. And then, reading *Zorka*, his goodness came through his characters, Pasha and Nina. I don't think an evil man would write a story that conveyed such goodness, nor would a truly good man want to write about evil."

Tetushka nodded. "It would seem a person's love or goodness is transcendent; and can transcend to others through one's writing, as well as through death?"

"Yes," Clara agreed.

"What have you learned, Annie?"

Annie's eyes teared up as she spoke. "We all have flaws, and are crippled one way or another, but it doesn't mean we can't love or be loved. It also made me feel just because God allowed me to lose my family, it doesn't mean He doesn't love me. Nina lost her family, but she still loved God and believed He was good. She also helped me understand we are all somehow connected by God's Spirit, even if we live in a different time and country."

"Like us meeting each other and reading this

story together," Clara added. "It gave us all something we needed from each other and from the writer."

"If both the writer and the characters in his story reflect this goodness, do you think the character, Pasha, was based on the author, Pavel?" Annie asked.

"I will tell you something," Tetushka replied. "In Russia, Pavel is the formal name for Pasha."

The girls looked at each other, wide-eyed. "So, he is Pasha!"

"And the story is true!"

"If the story is true, and Pavel really was Pasha, then, who was Nina?" Annie asked.

Tetushka took something from her coat pocket. With a tender smile, she laid a small wood rabbit at the foot of the grave marker. "Remember me," she whispered.

The End

Also available on audiobook at Audible or amazon

**Listen to it free with this code:
https://www.audible.com/pd/B0773
W7CV3/?source_code=AUDFPWS022318
9MWT-BK-ACX0-
100022&ref=acx_bty_BK_ACX0_100022_r
h_us**

**For more books by Renee Riva visit
Amazon.com or
www.reneeriva.com**

Renee's Amazon Author Central Page:

**https://www.amazon.com/Renee-
Riva/e/B001K8UJ52/ref=sr_ntt_srch_lnk_
1?qid=1548813822&sr=1-1**

29245498R00083

Made in the USA
San Bernardino, CA
13 March 2019